Storyteller

THREE /// OWLS
PUBLISHING

EDITORS
Lydia Silbernagel
Shay Shivecharan

COVER
Photographer: Jeannie Albers
Model: Darryl Pickett

 storytellermag.com

 info@storytellermag.com

 fb.com/storytellermagazine

 @storytellermagazine

---

Storyteller is a quarterly publication that celebrates truth through writing. In its pages, you will find poetry, fiction, and nonfiction, each piece an expression of truth as known or experienced by its creator.

JEANNIE ALBERS

jalbersstudio.com | jeannie@jalbersstudio.com

PORTRAIT - COMMERCIAL - STUDIO & LOCATION - LIFESTYLE - FASHION

POETRY

FICTION

NONFICTION

Authors

Darryl Pickett @flippyshark

Darryl has been a Show Writer for Walt Disney Imagineering, and continues to consult for the Mouse, and for many others in the theme park industry. His first novel, The Secret Feast of Father Christmas, was published in 2012, and his next on the way. He is also an actor, a playwright, a singer and songwriter. He aligns with Chaotic Good, and happily embraces his life of restless creativity.

Blake Slaughter @blakeeslaughter

Blake Slaughter, born in Orlando and raised in Clermont, Florida, has had a passion for writing since he was eleven. Envisioning stories of horror and drama, he took up writing and hasn't stopped. He attributes a lot of his inspiration to music- from Frank Sinatra to Led Zeppelin. Other inspirations include authors Stephen King and William Peter Blatty, poets Edgar Allen Poe and Walt Whitman- most notably his poem I Sing the Body Electric, and the American film director Stanley Kubrick.

Londyn Rayne @londynrayne

Londyn Rayne is a songwriter, lyricist, music producer, and a performing member in the band Sunset Roulett. She is also the founder of Orlando based ministry Label Me His. An advocate for mental/emotional health and healing, Londyn finds comfort in connecting with the power of words and expressing her pain and passions creatively whether it be through music, poetry or photography. She is soon releasing her first poetry collection and believes vulnerability is the beautiful beginning of transformation.

Aaron Morrison @theaaronmorrison

Aaron was born during the great ______natural disaster________ in the ____season____ of ____year____. He spends his free time exploring ________unusual location________ and raising domesticated _______fictional creature (plural)_______.One day, he would like to ______verb______ his way to ______place______ and try the various _____noun(plural)_____.

Lawrence Griffin @flightofgriffin

Lawrence Griffin was born in Orlando and raised on a steady diet of horror movies and books, which has contributed to his writing, along with much attention paid to the state of the world today. In his free time, he can be found at the movie theater or the beach. He's had stories published in Bards and Sages' Society of Misfit Stories, Hellbound Books and other local and online publications. He's also had journalism published in numerous papers and magazines.

Zarah Gates @zarah.noel

Most think Zara, but don't think the store. Think about a wanna-be vagabond, vegan, and Viking, all in one petite body. Someone you would find trumping around an abandoned sugar mill, or dressed up as a frat-boy dancing around screaming. But they'd also be found sitting staring at stars. If you find someone who is described liked this, you have found a Zarah; and this is your word of warning. You'll want to put her in a box, but don't, she fears confinement.

Authors

Lydia Silbernagel @lydiasilby

Lydia is a recent graduate of the University of Florida, where she studied English and Religion. She devotes most of her time to petting cats, making coffee, poring over books, and fulfilling any other English Major stereotype you could possibly imagine. Lydia's professors told her that her writing is "dull and uninspired," so she's decided to plumb the depths of her masochism by sharing said writing with the world.

Joshua Mahn @joshmahnwrites

Joshua Mahn is hosting a Yeti-flesh cook-off, Christmas Eve, under the usual bridge next to the mysterious shrine. $10 entry fee, all proceeds will go towards the liberation of the proletariat. Kumis, Chicha, and 7-Up will be provided.

Tanner Johns

Tanner Johns bartends in order to fund his goal to become the first tree-hugger to hug a tree on Mars. Wish him luck with that. He's afraid of heights. When he's not bartending, he's writing, drawing, reading about space, playing video games, or sleeping. Usually all at the same time. He's a cool guy

Seth Kaye @iamsethkaye

Seth Kaye is learning to be a poet. Though predisposed to the misconception that poetry is either world-alteringly legendary or utterly worthless (with no space in between), he has tasked himself with cultivating the elusive terrain in the middle. Devoted to the art of songwriting, Seth has only recently allowed himself to indulge in the writing of poems sans musical accompaniment. fueled by a passion for language and the lyrical expression of human experience and emotion, he is on his way.

Gabriel McLeod @gabrielmcleod

Gabriel McLeod hails from a southern town intersected by railroads and rivers, canopied by magnolia and moonlight. He was born from a family of hard workers, dreamers and story tellers. He currently is working on a collection of short stories, a book of poetry and the beginning stages of a novel. Gabriel made Orlando his home for over 20 years and proudly lives with two extraordinary daughters and two enigmatic cats in a house with full bookshelves in every room.

THERE'S NEVER BEEN SUCH A SKY
BY DARRYL PICKETT

Photography by Victor Gibbs

December, 1977
Santa Fe, New Mexico

The sunsets in New Mexico are famous for their brilliant primary colors, for being immense, and painterly. In Santa Fe, these fantastic kaleidoscopes appear over the rooftops of earthy adobe houses and church buildings. In December, paper-bag *farolitos* limn the sidewalks, their glow creating candle-lit trails along the sidewalks and roadways, guiding the eye from foreground to subject to blazing celestial backdrop. Generations of painters and photographers have tried to recapture the spectacle. The best have come close, but there is simply no substitute for witnessing it yourself.

In 1977, I spent the season wrapped in its sensory delights. Not just the bold brushstrokes of evening sky, but the smoke and rugged fragrance of piñon and cedar from kiva fireplaces. The anise-enhanced taste of *biscochitos*, and the decadent joy of a caramel apple. (From Señor Murphy's, the finest candy-maker in the Southwest.) Just enough chill in the air to wake the senses and justify the wearing of cozy sweaters or jaunty jackets, in which clothing I always felt more confident, more fully myself.

I sensed then, as I can confirm now, that it was a privilege to spend those weeks in such an evocative place. With so many splendid people.

At twelve years old, I still sang soprano. It was easily the thing I was best known and most praised for. In particular, grown-ups expressed their admiration for my talents, and that always rocketed my sense of worth a mile high. I enjoyed believing I was an early bloomer, already smart, and accomplished. My voice was the gift that caused other smart, accomplished people to talk to me.

A number of favorite adults granted me this kindness, treating me like a peer. I remember and remain grateful to them. They allowed me to exist in a state of happy illusion. I was in a hurry to vault over adolescence and land comfortably into an identity of admirable adult person, fully formed, brilliant but kind. That this did not happen will surprise no one, though it eventually came as quite a shock to me.

That year, I was cast in the lead role of the famous Christmas opera, *Amahl and the Night Visitors*, composed by Gian Carlo Menotti. The story is a simple one. Amahl is a shepherd boy, living with his mother in a humble abode somewhere along the road to Bethlehem. The Three Kings arrive and ask to stay the night as they rest from their travels following the Christmas star. Amahl is disabled, needing a crutch to walk. He and his mother live in poverty, but by the end of the one-act opera, a Christmas miracle occurs and young Amahl is able to join the kings on their journey so he can give thanks to the Christ-child in person.

At that time in my life, I had been singing in different boys choirs and children's choirs ever since the age of seven. I had been decisively bitten by the show business bug. The role of Amahl promised a chance for me to shine, not only as a singer, but as an actor, in a role tailor-made to evoke sympathy and sentimental emotions. I relished it.

The theater stood out on the Old Pecos Trail, close enough to the city center to be convenient, remote enough to seem like wonderfully private, a well-kept secret. The building housed an art museum and a performance space, and was my second home for a span of seven or eight weeks. Best of all for me, it was easy enough to duck out the back door during breaks and gaze up at the enormous, gorgeous sky, and believe that its splendor was being assembled just for me.

But a sky of nearly equal enchantment existed indoors. The scenic backdrop for the show featured a night sky assembled from white Christmas tree lights poking through black material, with the iconic Christmas star projected from the booth at the back of the house. It was technically primitive, but so artfully created that it astonished everyone when it was first shown to us with the house lights down. It created a believable night sky that seemed miles away from the back wall of the stage, a magnificent illusion. A simple silhouette of desert horizon, a plaster hillside and dirt path, and the detailed and realistic interior of the shepherd boy's home completed the setting. All by itself, it was postcard perfect, worth the price of admission, with its storybook first-century appeal, its warmth and evocative, inviting sense of depth.

I could marvel at this interior vista with nearly the same wonder that I gazed on the God-provided panorama outside.

At the beginning of the opera, my character, the young boy Amahl, sings to his mother about that miraculous night sky.

> *Damp clouds have shined it, and soft winds have swept it,*
> *As if to make it ready for a king's ball*

The composer Menotti was justly famous for fitting melody to his own beautiful lyrics with precision and flawless prosody. The tuneful notes did most of the acting for me. I couldn't help but sound excited, entranced and engaged, while singing those melodies.

> *All its lanterns are lit, all its torches are burning*

Every moment I spent on that stage, I was in its world, lost to all else. Those dime-store stars were real. My crutch was needed. I was Amahl. My stage mother, angelically beautiful and peerlessly gifted, was Amahl's mother. The reality of it was complete and true.

I was surrounded by people I knew. Many in the chorus of shepherds and shepherdesses were part of an adult choir, and they were the parents of kids who I sang alongside in a parallel children's choir. Their familiar, faces, their familial presence, leant comfort, and confirmed my place at the center of an obviously charmed life.

One of the three kings was played by the director of those choirs; a stubborn, inspiring, aggravating man who loomed so large in that segment of my life, he would require another longer, more troubled remembrance. He rests now in the tranquility of those magnificent stars.

My mother was also in the cast, dancing alongside a magnificent elf of a man, a choreographer and artist with legit Broadway and Hollywood credentials.

Mom's presence anchored the entire enterprise, allowing me the advantage of comfort and security, all while having permission to test my wings. She loved the music as much as I did. On our drive from Los Alamos to Santa Fe, we once played the Shepherd's Dance on the car's cassette player, and she got so carried away with its ebullient spirit, she didn't notice that we were soon speeding, nearing 80 miles an hour.

Forty-three years later, those memories are vivid. But they are no longer separated into individual performances, distinct days and nights. The entirety of it plays in my mind as if it had taken place over one extended, impossible evening. It's a movie, lengthy but wondrous, though playing with its reels out of order.

There are highlights, specific scenes that stand out, not always not always complete, not always accurate, but lucid.

My picture appeared in several newspapers, proof positive that my intuition of pending fame and significance were correct. And there were reviews. One of them described my voice as *"incredibly strong and clear,"* and those four words became a caption and a tagline.

But in truth, those words were followed by, "... *though Mr. Pickett's voice sometimes cracked on the higher notes, a sign that his upper register may be facing the inevitability of age"* And it was true. My voice had begun to change. I fought it with every ounce of will that I had. Because this work, this role, this time and place, were so perfect, so absolutely where I belonged. And those changes meant this state of grace was temporal.

Was it ever.

But for now, I sat with my family in a restaurant having a pre-show dinner. My grandfather, my aunt and uncle sat with us, ready to come see the show later that evening. And our waiter recognized me. He had seen the show, and he shouted out, with charming mispronunciation, "Hey! That's *AY*-mahl!" (This survived as a family catch phrase for a good long while.) I beamed at the recognition.

In fact, it boosted my exuberance so much, as the meal ended, I stepped outside and danced and jumped with happy exuberance. I literally bounced off the outer adobe walls of the Inn at Loretto. And I got roundly chastised by a security guard who saw my unbridled, careless excesses.

Backstage, as I joked with friends, and got into costume, and wallowed in the joyful rightness of belonging there, the choir director, that man who held such eminence he was akin to a second father, approached me, looking worried.

"Your grandfather had a heart attack," he told me. "Your mother is at the hospital with him. She probably won't be able to dance in the show tonight."

And the sheer fantasy and perfection of it all fell away, replaced by panic and worry. And somewhere, an immature resentment that circumstances had thrown imperfection into my joyous moment.

In the time-fluid edit that plays in my mind, this news is joined by word that the musicians in the orchestra might not play, that they are negotiating for better pay, and may strike. The show might have to go on with simple piano accompaniment, instead of the small but full-sounding orchestra that had accompanied my every step and song up to then.

And so within my treasured story-memory, there is a time of tension, complaint, and concern. There is talk the show could close before the end of its run. And far worse, I have a scary reality to face, a family member in hospital, in danger. And I have to go on anyway, and evoke the same wonder that came so naturally every other night, even as my confidence and world are shaking from these jolts.

And the dawning awareness that life is fragile, happiness is temporal. The show has to go on, but the spotlight is fickle. Crisis can happen at any time.

At this long remove, I can no longer remember the order in which these things occurred, or how far into the run of the show. But they sit in the story just ahead of the denouement. Oversimplified, but true all the same. Everything worked out.

My mother somehow made it to the performance. And my grandfather, though he did not see the show, nevertheless recovered and was able to return home not long after that particular scare. There were still some years before our family had to face the reality which that situation portended. Gratitude for what time we still had, for the love, concern and care my family gave me, that I took for granted, that I now acknowledge.

And the orchestra did not strike, did not sit out any of the shows. Thanks from decades later to them, for keeping up the rich score of this chapter of my life.

So, those were the incursions from the churn of ever-troubled life, In spite of them, I got to live out the rest of that enchanted spell. If I press play, I hear it in perfect surround sound. The lilting overture begins, with the string section singing out Menotti's gorgeous lyrical introduction, the oboe then picking out the tune played by Amahl on his shepherd's pipe.

This serenade invokes that amazing sky, an all-encompassing cinematic hybrid, combining two splendid realities; the skillfully made theatrical backdrop and the boundless expanse of a Santa Fe December night. The Christmas star burns above it all with divine ferocity, and I sing to it.

"It moves across the sky like a chariot on fire"

For a brief time, everything is perfect. I have gifts to bring. Impermanent gifts, and a voice about to deepen, a childhood about to shift into troubled, confused teenager-hood.

But not yet. For now, I live for a while in that suspended moment. Life is suffused with divine music. I have certainty, belief, optimism, and comfort.

None of those things endure steadily, nor can they. But the memory is sustaining. For as long as I have it, for as much as I can use words to share some sense of it. There was no better Christmas. There was no more loving family nor more supportive community. There was no luckier child. How glad I am to still know that.

CELATUS DIABOLI

BY AARON MORRISON

Celatus Diaboli is the winner of Storyteller's 2nd annual
Scary Owl Challenge Writing Contest

Eliza had to have it

As soon as she saw it, she knew it was the one. Pristine. Silken. Glistening like fine, soft strands of obsidian. It looked more beautiful than any jewelry Eliza had ever seen. And this adornment, at least to her, was more valuable.It wasn't that Eliza was particularly a vain person. At first, in fact, she had been mostly uncomfortable with the idea of purchasing a wig.

She had dealt with a form of Grave's disease and hyperthyroidism her whole life, managing it, and never using it as an excuse for anything in her life. Eliza had always kept her condition to herself when possible. She didn't want anyone feeling sorry for her, or treating her like she was some kind of invalid. In recent months, however, she had developed alopecia areata which had begun aggressively attacking her hair follicles, and it became difficult to hide such an obvious, and outward, effect.

It was Eliza's best friend that had suggested looking into getting a wig.

"Eliza. Girl. It wouldn't hurt just to look." Bethany had said. "I mean, you're going to be beautiful any way you decide to go. Bald. Headwraps. Hats. Wigs. I just think you should explore all your options."

So now Eliza was looking to purchase the most beautiful thing, wig or otherwise, she had ever seen.

The odd thing was, Eliza had not even been out today with the intent of shopping for a wig. She had simply been out checking the various second hand shops and curio stores. There was barely any intent of necessarily purchasing anything at all. Sometimes something interesting would catch her eye and, if she could get a good deal, she would buy whatever trinket or clothing item that would cause some gleeful conversation and admiration from her and her friends.

In an almost dreamlike state Eliza approached the register with her find. Eliza had a brief and quiet thought of confusion as to her current actions and state of mind. But whatever personal reflection was brewing was quickly squelched by the overwhelming need to purchase the wig.

"That'll be one hundred dollars."

"Oh. Yeah. Right." Eliza realized, in her eagerness, she hadn't even checked the price. She pulled her credit card out of her purse, and handed it to the woman behind the counter. *100 isn't bad,* she thought. *Especially for a human hair wig.* Eliza wasn't sure why she had made that assumption. "Do you know anything about this wig?"

"I'm sure I don't darlin'," the plump old woman replied as she swiped Eliza's card. She handed the card back to Eliza, and turned the point-of-sale device around so Eliza could sign the screen. The digital device seemed very much out of place, given the nature of the store. "Items come and go here. Some have stories, some do not. It's hard to keep track sometimes." She smiled as she handed a bag containing the box holding the carefully placed wig.

Eliza hadn't even noticed that the woman had so deftly removed the wig from the mannequin head and packed the wig up. There had been a brief moment that she swore her signature on the screen had turned red, but she chalked it up to a trick of the light.

"Thank you!" Eliza raised her hand in brief wave as she turned to leave.

"Of course, darlin'. Enjoy!"

Once she was home, Eliza prepared to try on the wig. With the same excitement that a child has on Christmas morning, Eliza could not wait to put on the wig. She put a wig liner, made a few adjustments, then placed the wig, hair forward, on her head. She flipped her head back, sending the obsidian strands flowing back and down.

It was perfect.

Eliza, with no experience, somehow had the wig fitted and placed perfectly on her first attempt. And it looked...

Oh my god, Eliza thought, *I look good!*

Eliza had never been one to preen in front of the mirror, but she couldn't help but admire her reflection. Her default state of self consciousness soon took back control, and Eliza felt a little silly. She hesitated, however, when she went to remove the wig. Eliza did not want to take it off, but, after a brief moment of struggle, did.

Eliza then realized she didn't have a mannequin head to properly store the wig, and was moderately annoyed with herself for not just asking to purchase the one it was on in the vintage store.

Eliza verified her uncertain recall that there was a costume shop not that far from her apartment. After calling to make sure they had one for sale, Eliza put on a ball cap and set out for the shop. It wasn't too far to walk, so she did, as that was her personal favorite mode of transportation. She found her thoughts returning to the wig on the way there and back. Eliza wasn't sure how she felt about these minor, but borderline obsessive, thoughts about her new purchase, but she dismissed them as just being excited and nervous about such a new endeavour.

Once home again, she carefully placed the wig on the mannequin head, and smoothed out the hair. Even on the plastic blank face it looked gorgeous. Eliza managed to pull herself away from doting on the wig to fix herself dinner, which she enjoyed with a glass of wine and her favorite show on the television.

"So, I did it." Eliza had called Bethany to tell her about the day's big purchase. "I got a wig."

"You did? Must have been amazing. I know you and your picky ways." Bethany laughed.

"Shut up." Eliza laughed as well. "But yeah. It's like, I dunno. Perfect."

"You'll have to wear it Friday night then."

"Maybe." There was some hesitation in Eliza's voice.

"Eliza Constance," Bethany scolded, "don't you dare try and weasel out of going. We always go to Trouvere's, and this Friday is no exception."

"Alright, alright!" Eliza laughed. "I'll be there."

"You better!"

"Bye!" Eliza feigned annoyance.

"See you!"

Eliza's sleep that night was intermittent. She woke up several times throughout the night, with the vauguest hints of possible dreams. The only image Eliza could recall was something about a field. She was sure there was more, but it was dancing just beyond her memory, as dreams are wont to do. Eliza rolled over and snuck in whatever last few moments of sleep she could while the wigged mannequin head watched silently from the top of her vanity.

***

"Damn, Eliza! You look hot!" Bethany was always one to gas up her friends, but there was an extra dash of sincere surprise in her voice when she saw Eliza.

"Stop it!" Eliza responded with her standard self conscious, nervous laugh. Eliza wasn't wearing anything different than she normally wore when they were going out to Trouvere's, but even she, though she wouldn't have admitted it, felt more attractive than usual. Eliza was pretty, kept in shape, but never dressed with the intent of looking "provocative" or "sexy". Cute, yes, but never beyond that. But she had definitely felt sexier tonight. The only difference tonight was the wig. Eliza thought it might have just been a confidence boost from the perfection of the obsidian locks that cascaded over her neck and shoulders, but, regardless of the reason, she definitely felt more attractive.

"So what's the over/under on free drink offers tonight? I'm gonna put it at," Bethany looked Eliza up and down, "three and a half."

While offers of "buy you a drink?" weren't unusual, the vast numbers of lustful, or few genuinely nice, men being ever present, Bethany's prediction seemed unusually high. They always got offers, though Bethany always got more than Eliza. Bethany was the "hot" friend, while Eliza was the "cute and sweet" friend. Plus, Eliza tended to turn down any drink offers, albeit with a polite "no, thank you," while Bethany tended to accept.

"It would be rude to refuse a gift," Bethany would say jokingly.

"You know, they usually aren't offering out of the goodness of their hearts, right?" Eliza would respond.

"Well, they shouldn't offer then. It's not a gift if you expect something in return."

"I'm sure they all understand that concept." Laughing sarcasm.

"Then they better learn."

Trouvere's was a jazz and blues club that was the local hotspot for anyone that didn't really enjoy the dance club scene, or didn't want to go to the major bar chains. The quality of the music and the drinks were always high, and the atmosphere tended to be a lot more chill than other places. Though avoiding the hookup culture was virtually impossible, Trouvere's was better than most in being left alone when you turned someone down.

Eliza immediately felt eyes on her. She was definitely being checked out, by both men and women alike. Eliza somehow felt both uncomfortable and excited by the attention. She wasn't sure if it was always like this, or if she was just more aware of it tonight. Either way, she was here to enjoy her night with friends, and that's what she was going to do.

Eliza and Bethany joined the small group they were there to meet. They occupied a few of the small round tables that peppered the club. There wasn't a bad seat in the house, these just happened to be far enough back to enjoy the music, but still manage some level of conversation. Eliza and Bethany, drinks in hand, greeted their friends with the usual smiles, hellos, and hugs, and sat down. Their small group of now eight, was an even mix of guys and gals, including Darren. Eliza had met Darren a few times before, as he was a friend of a friend of Bethany's. Eliza found him attractive, and found his quiet, though quick witted, ways intriguing. He seemed genuinely kind and shy, and their friends always had good things to say about him. Eliza and Darren greeted each other with smiles, a wave, and a "hey!"

Bethany, who had been encouraging Eliza to go after Darren, gave Eliza a little nudge and a wink, who responded with widening eyes and silent mouthing of "stop!"

The drink offers started pretty quickly, with, at least it seemed to Eliza, every time she went up to the bar, whether to get a drink herself or just to walk up with Bethany or another of their friends. Three men and one woman, fulfilling the "over" on Bethany's prediction.

"Buy me a drink?"

"What?" Eliza laughed, half confused looking up at Darren, who had joined her up at the bar.

"I just figured I'd mix it up." His own self consciousness starting to show. "I, mmm, stupid dad joke. Sorry."

"No no no!" Eliza put her hand on his arm. "It was funny! I was just in my own world."

Darren smiled, a bit more at ease.

"Do you know this band?" Eliza gestured towards the stage.

"Yeah, actually. I mean, I'm about to sound like 'that guy,' but I saw them a few years back. The Light Hands. Really good psychedelic blues rock band out of Tennessee. Knowing a bunch of overly specific musical genres is kinda my thing." Darren coated the last statement in joking feigned pride.

Eliza laughed. "Well, good, because I know nothing about music. Well, other than if I like it or not."

They finally got their drinks and returned to the tables. Bethany, in full "wingman" mode, had moved seats so Eliza and Darren sat next to each other when they got back. They continued chatting, with Darren occasionally getting distracted by a song the band would play, which Eliza found endearing. They did manage to exchange numbers before a hug goodbye at the end of the night.

"So?" Bethany dragged out the questioning word. "Spill it."

"What?" Eliza laughed.

Bethany shrugged and gestured in a "seriously?" exasperated manner.

Eliza failed to suppress her smile. "We are going to go to that Tuesday Night Food Truck Rally thing this week."

"Yes! Look at you, all confident and shit!"

"It's just a date."

"Mmmhmm"

"You are terrible!"

***

Once home, Eliza took off the wig, though she was reluctant to do so. She still felt it strange she was having such an attachment to a wig, of all things. Eliza figured the current fondness was exacerbated by the confidence it had seemed to give her. Regardless, she set the wig on the mannequin head, brushed out the locks, though it did not seem to need it, and then undressed and took a shower. Soon enough, she was in bed, relaxed from the shower, and sleepy from the late night and alcohol. Sleep came. And so did dreams.

A field. The same field as before. Bare feet on the grass. She could feel the moisture on the dark green and gray blades. A forest encompassed the outer reaches of the field. Their imposing, and mostly leafless, arms reaching towards the foreboding dark and cloudy dusk sky. A figure stood in the distance.

Eliza awoke. Her sharp intake of air and pounding heart startled her.

She evened her breathing and settled herself down. Eliza was uncertain why the dream had frightened her so. The moon had perfectly placed itself in the sky to send light through the bedroom window, casting a silvery blue spotlight on the mannequin head. The light seemed to slowly cascade down the fibers of obsidian hair, like some etheriel waterfall. Eliza stared back into the blank eye divots of the mannequin head. Finally breaking her gaze, Eliza turned over to try and find sleep again. She could feel that it would now be elusive. Accepting defeat for that moment, Eliza decided to get out of bed, make herself a cup of tea, and finish the night on the couch with a ceramic mug of herbal tea and a show. Sleep eventually returned to her, their apparent quarrel over, and they spent the rest of the mercifully dreamless night together on the couch.

***

Tuesday Night Food Truck Rally was a success. Eliza found conversation with Darren easy and enjoyable. Even the silent moments were pleasant, and not the brutal awkwardness of one person trying to carry the conversation, or neither person having anything to say. The food was good. The company was better. Though whatever local musician they had performing wasn't good at all. It was a fun and refreshing evening for both of them, despite the soundtrack of bad Tom Petty, Beatles, and Jeff Buckley covers. The night ended with a hug and kiss goodnight, and the promise and eagerness to see each other again soon. Which they did. Dates and time together. Fridays at Trouvere's. The official social media status. Beautiful, and mutually satisfying love making. Those months of their blossoming relationship were like a high for both of them.

It bothered Darren some that Eliza seemed to be constantly wearing the wig, and he did try to broach the subject with Eliza. She had responded harshly, snapping at Darren to not tell her "what to fucking do."

"Whoa, whoa!" Darren put his hands up. "I didn't it mean it like that. Look, I love *you*, Eliza. You don't always have to hide what you are going through from me." He gestured to his own head. "I dunno. I'm probably saying this super shittily. Obviously."

Eliza, having returned back to normal, was almost in tears, ashamed for having gone at Darren so harshly. "I'm sorry. I don't know what's wrong with me lately." Eliza had been uncharacteristically short tempered with pretty much everyone the past few weeks. She hadn't been able to quite peg what was wrong. She was happier than ever, but also angrier. She was unequivocally, and unexplainably, healthier than ever, but also, at times, felt sicker than she had ever been.

"Hey, hey." Darren put his arms around Eliza, who embraced him back. "Whatever's going on, we'll get through it."

They swayed gently back. Eliza looked up at Darren. "I don't deserve you."

"Now *that's* bullshit." Darren smirked.

They both smiled and laughed. They let out a mutual sigh as Eliza returned to resting her head against Darren's chest. She couldn't see the concern on Darren's face as they stood swaying in the embrace.

***

Another Friday, another night at Trouvere's. A new band was playing. The Latin and Island infused jazz blues swirled through the air. The male and female shared lead vocals, danced, and parried deftly, adding even more brightness and sensuality to the music.

Eliza had gone up to the bar. Looking back, she saw Bethany talking to Darren. He was leaning forward, hand on the back of Bethany's chair, eyes slightly squinted, gently nodding as he listened intently to whatever Bethany was saying.

Bitch. Eliza was shocked at the viciousness of the jealousy in her thought. She closed her eyes and shook her head briefly as if to toss the thoughts away. Eyes open again, she saw Bethany talking and laughing with the rest of their friends. Darren was walking to the restroom.

Eliza turned her attention back to the bar, resuming her wait for one of the two bartenders.

"Buy you a drink?"

Eliza looked at the man who had made the offer.

"I'm here with someone," Eliza responded. "Besides, even if I wasn't, do you think I'm going to owe you something because you bought me a drink?"

"Nope. Just like to buy beautiful women drinks." He then proceeded to order two gin and tonics. The man picked up one of the glasses, clinked it against the remaining one, before raising his briefly to Eliza and walking off.

Eliza stared down at the drink on the bar momentarily before a familiar voice broke her daze.

"Free drink?" Darren had returned from the restroom, and witnessed the tail end of the exchange as he had walked up.

"Something like that."

Darren pointed at the drink and shrugged a "why not?" when one of the bartenders approached for his order. Once completed, Darren switched out the drinks, giving Eliza the fresh one and taking the other. He sipped it, grimacing slightly at the taste of tonic water and juniper.

They drank in relative silence. Eliza eventually slipped her arm through Darren's, and laid her head against his shoulder as a slow, but heavy, blues song played.

"I need to talk to you, bitch." The slurred, angry words of an obviously drunk woman shattered the moment.

"Excuse me?" Eliza turned, shocked and confused.

"I wanna know why you were talking to my man."

Darren had started to move forward, but Eliza put her hand against his chest to stop him.

"Listen clearly you stupid bitch. 'Your man' approached me, so why don't you go yell at him about why he's buying drinks for other women, or why he can't keep his dick in his pants. Go bother someone else you ignorant drunk." Eliza felt like she was observing from within, listening to someone else speak through her.

The woman stammered in anger, and stepped forward, intending to swing on Eliza.

"Os perdere." Eliza spoke, her voice simultaneously sounding like her own but also not.

As the woman made her first step, her ankle gave way as soon as it touched the floor. A snapping sound pierced through the music, followed by a nightmarish scream of pain.

The woman was now on the floor, her tibia broken and piercing through her flesh.

Eliza, back to herself, was in horrified shock at what she was witnessing.

Darren was in shock as well, though it was mixed with a kind of awe at Eliza defending herself, though her words might have gone too far.

The rest of the night was a blur. Eliza answered questions from the police as emergency services tended to the woman. All witnesses, including the security footage, confirmed the other woman had been the aggressor, and Eliza had not touched the woman in any way. The woman was heavily intoxicated, and the most simple explanation was that she had simply stepped wrong, lost her balance in the most unlucky way, resulting in the fracture.

Eliza nodded, barely taking in what the policewoman was telling her. Eliza was silent as Darren drove her home.

"Are you sure you don't want me to stay?"

"I just. I just need to be alone. Okay?"

"Okay." Darren nodded in reluctant understanding. "Call me, obviously, if you need anything."

"I will."

"I'll, uh, I'll call you in the morning."

Eliza nodded.

"Love you."

"Love you." Eliza mumbled as she slowly and robotically shut the door.

Darren lingered outside the door for a moment, uncertain of what to do. Frustrated at his inability to help, he turned away and went home.

A field. Bare feet on the grass. She could feel the moisture on the dark green and gray blades. A forest encompassed the outer reaches of the field, their imposing and mostly leafless arms reaching towards the foreboding dark and cloudy dusk sky. A figure stood in the distance.

A woman. Naked, save a thin black robe that hung loosely and open over her shoulders. The decapitated head of a large goat covered her own, masking her face. Crimson had run down her neck and breasts. Long, obsidian black hair cascaded from under the goat head, and over the figure's shoulders.

Eliza continued to walk towards her, compelled to approach.

Eliza, now only a few feet from the woman, watched as she removed the goat head, revealing her beautiful, wicked, blood-soaked face. The woman discarded the goat head, stepping forward, letting the robe fall to the ground as she did. Her hand reached around the back of Eliza's head, pulling her forward, kissing her. Eliza tasted the iron of the blood that was on the woman's lips and tongue. Eliza tried to pull away, but she felt her skin had become fused to the woman's. She struggled in panic, but Eliza was pulled further into the woman, who had Eliza in full embrace. The two merged like some reverse mitosis, leaving the woman alone in the field, standing naked and smiling.

Eliza woke up hyperventilating. She looked around her room in a panic, her eyes finally resting on a moonlit, bare mannequin head. Eliza's hands went instinctively up to her own head and discovered the wig still on. Eliza figured, in the shock of the events of the night, she had forgotten to take it off before bed.

After turning on the bedroom light, Eliza sat down in front of the vanity to properly remove the wig. Bringing her hands up to the sides of her head, her fingertips ran through her hair instead of catching the edge of the wig to lift it off. Confused, Eliza tried again. The same results. She stood, the chair falling backwards, and leaned towards the vanity mirrors. Looking. Searching. There was no seam. No lip to lift. Only folicels and her own skin.

Afraid, and unsure, Eliza rushed to her bathroom. She grabbed a pair of scissors and began cutting away at the hair.

Snip. Snip. Snip! Snipsnipsnip!

Eliza attacked the many fine strands furiously. She'd worry about making it look nice later. She just wanted to cut it back as far as she dared go. Eliza didn't know how else to rid herself of it, and in the moment, this was all she had. The deed complete, she set the scissors down, turned on the faucet, and leaned down to splash water on her face.

The water felt good on her skin, and brought about the briefest moments of relief. She felt light, silken strands caressing her neck and shoulders. Shaking, Eliza looked up at the mirror and discovered her head still covered fully in long, perfect hair. The clippings that should have been on the floor were gone. Eliza collapsed in a corner of her bathroom and sobbed until she fell asleep.

***

Eliza stood outside the second hand shop, or rather, what used to be the second hand shop where she purchased the wig. She had ignored Darren's and Bethany's calls, as well as Darren's "Good morning, babe. How are you feeling?" and Bethany's "Checking in on you" texts.

Eliza had set out in the morning and was now in front of an empty storefront, with little evidence that anything had been occupying the space at all. Eliza had tried the front door, and looked inside, hand cupped around her eye and pressed against the glass as if searching would somehow bring the store to life, or prove she was mistaken in her observation that the store was closed and empty.

Her frustration gave way to resignation, which then gave way to an eerie peace. There were things she wanted, no, needed, to get, and she had all day to do it.

***

It was Sunday evening when Eliza finally returned Darren's phone calls.

"Hey! Babe! Been trying to reach you all weekend! Are you okay?" Darren was relieved to finally hear from her.

"I'm fine, my love. Why wouldn't I be?"

"I mean, it's been a, uh, unusual weekend."

"Let's go out tonight."

"Uh, yeah, sure! Where do you want to go?"

"Trouvere's."

"Really?" Darren couldn't mask his surprise in her choice.

"Pick me up in an hour."

"Yeah, right, sure." Darren paused. "Are you sure you're okay?"

"See you soon." Eliza hung up.

An hour later, Eliza greeted Darren with a deep kiss outside her apartment building. Her lips had a faint taste of herbs and honey, and Eliza was leading Darren to his car before he could fully process the thought.

Once at Trouvere's, they made their way directly to the bar. There were a few sideways glances from patrons, and a mildly surprised look from the bartender that had been there Friday night. Darren responded to a puzzled look the bartender gave him with an "I'm not sure either" shrug.

Eliza ordered two bourbons, neat, handed one to Darren, clinked her glass against his, and had her drink downed by the time Darren had finished his second sip. Eliza nodded her head in perfect time to the music and waited for Darren to finish his drink. As Darren neared his last sip, drinking a little faster than he normally would have, Eliza ordered two more. It seemed to Darren that the energy of Trouvere's was dulling, and only Eliza was in focus. The second drink done, Eliza's lips were on Darren's again. While the couple hadn't shied away from public displays of affection, this was much more than their usual hand holding or a light kiss on the top of the head. Eliza's fingertips lightly caressed the back of Darren's head, her honeyed lips and tongue intertwined with his.

"Let's get out of here."

Darren, while still confused at Eliza's current brazenness, was, in no uncertain terms, aroused. After leaving enough cash on the bar to pay for the drinks and give a generous tip, Darren, being lead by the hand, followed Eliza out of Trouvere's.

It had begun to rain on their way back to Eliza's apartment, and their clothes were soaked, dripping water on to the floor of her living room. Darren had just enough time to take in the extraordinary amount of dried herbs and flowers hanging about the apartment. Before he could make a comment on Eliza's new choice of decor, her mouth was on his again, and her hands began to deftly remove his clothing.

Eliza had turned them around and began guiding them into the bedroom, still kissing and undressing. Now in the bedroom, Eliza pushed Darren's naked form onto the bed and finished removing her own clothes. The candlelight danced over Eliza's wet, naked body, and cascaded down her black hair.

The candles had been lit hours ago. The melting wax continued to drip down, building the warm stalagmites at the base of the candles. The slowly flowing wax seemed to move in time with the drops of water that trickled down Eliza's body.

Eliza was on top of Darren, having put him inside her. Her hands brought Darren's hands to her breasts. Her sexual aggressiveness was both disconcerting and tantalizing. The sounds of their pleasure mixed with the sound of the rain as it battered against the window. She moved Darren's hands down to her hips, as her hands slid up his stomach to his chest. Eliza's fingernails dug down into Darren's chest, piercing the skin.

"Damn! Shit!" Darren flinched and grimaced. He started to push himself up, but Eliza's left hand was now around his throat, pushing him back down.

Eliza's movements became more intense and forceful, as did her cries of ecstasy. She was leaning forward now, left hand on Darren's throat, and her right hand next to the pillow. The sexual energy rose to its peak, and, in the throws of mutual climax, Eliza brought the knife, which she had hidden under the pillow, across Darren's throat.

Darren's eyes were wide as he gasped his final gurgling breaths, blood spurting from the wound.

Eliza leaned back, back arched, and ran her now blood covered hand down her lips, neck, and breasts. The energy of sex, blood, and sacrifice filling her like a drug, as euphoric a feeling as the orgasm that had immediately preceded it.

Her body relaxed. She sighed in satisfaction and steadied herself with hands on Darren's lifeless chest.

Eliza opened her eyes and recoiled in horror. Her shaking hands covering her mouth, stifling a scream she was too shocked to release. She fell off the bed, crawling back towards it, sobbing. One hand covering her mouth as the other touched Darren's face, as if it would dispel the nightmare. That's what this had to be.

She retreated to the bathroom, attempting to wash the blood from her body. Her hands shook. She sobbed and retched. Not knowing what else to do in her dazed condition, she put on some clothes and headed to Bethany's place.

Bethany, after looking through the peephole to see who was banging so loudly at her door, let Eliza inside. The rain had washed away most of the remaining blood from Eliza's face and hands, but some remained. Her eyes sunken, skin pale, Eliza collapsed to her knees only a few steps inside Bethany's home.

"Eliza! What's wrong? Tell me." Bethany spoke kindly as she knelt next to Eliza, hand on her shoulder, the other rubbing her back, desperately trying to comfort her friend and to find out what was going on.

"Darren... I... I think I hurt him." Eliza started sobbing again.

"Eliza. Please. Talk to me. Where's Darren? What happened to him?"

"Why do you care? Are you fucking him?" Eliza's voice angry and jealous and not quite her own.

"What the fuck, Eliza."

"I'm.. I'm sorry..." Eliza broke down again. "I don't know what's going on, Beth. What's wrong with me?"

Bethany helped her friend up, and guided her to the couch. "Eliza... Look at me... Breathe, okay? In... Out... In... Out..." Eliza calmed enough for Bethany to feel comfortable stepping away for a moment to grab some towels, dry clothes, and her cellphone. "I'll be right back, okay? We are gonna figure this out, okay?"

Eliza nodded in response.

"Okay. Be right back."

Bethany went to her bedroom, grabbed a pair of pajama pants and a top, a few towels from the closet, and put her phone in the pocket of her own pajama pants. "Okay. Let's get you dry, and..." Bethany's words trailed off as she saw Eliza standing in the kitchen with the large knife drawn from the knife block, and now in her hand.

"Eliza? Sweetie? What are you doing?" Bethany's concern mingled with fear in her voice.

"I... I have to stop this."

"Eliza, please... put that down. We can talk about whatever is..."

"No! It won't help!" Eliza's shout was desperate. Too many thoughts. Too many images. She could feel and hear the hair moving and growing on her head. She rushed towards Bethany.

Bethany, instinctively shifting to her right, was knocked further out the way as Eliza sprinted past her. Bethany heard the bathroom door slam shut and the click of the lock.

"Eliza! Eliza!" Bethany shouted and pounded her fist against the bathroom door. She slammed her shoulder into the door, which hurt her shoulder more than it made the door budge. Bethany kept banging on the door as she called 911.

The EMTs arrived first. One of them was able to kick in the bathroom door on the second attempt. They found Eliza curled up on the floor, the bloody knife laying near her where it had been dropped. The EMTs, while they began to treat Eliza, found it strange that, despite the blood and gore of her now severed and exposed scalp, and the pain she had to have been in, had a look of relief on her blood and tear stained face.

***

"That'll be one hundred dollars," said the plump older woman from behind the counter.

"Gimme one sec..." said the young woman as she searched for her debit card in her purse. "...and here you go!" She smiled as she handed over her card.

The mannequin head on the counter watched silently, the long obsidian locks of the wig it wore flowing down like a waterfall of midnight.

HOW ABOUT YOU MEET ME THERE

BY GABRIEL MCLEOD

How about I meet you on the moon one day?

I'll be there in some sort of rocking chair, counting the stars until you get there.

Maybe I'll have my slingshot to shoot moonrocks

Out into the quantum ripples, skipping out into space.

Earth will be there out in the background and I'll feel good

Knowing you're there while I wait.

I'll be fine, sifting my toes through the sparkling moondust, in the cold.

You know I was never crazy about the sun anyway.

There are so many places we have shared, so many places we could meet:

Down by the beach, up in the mountains,

Underneath a willow tree in the middle of a summer shower,

On the side of the road, listening to a chorus of crickets while stars fall

and we have no destination but a hundred miles of road.

Maybe on a boat in a bay or on a pier at sunset or maybe, simply,

On a corner on Then and When there is a laughter and smiles

And we reach to touch fingers and even lips.

So... If we never get to pick a place when this life is over and we forget how to keep in touch,

Let us meet on the moon one day.

I'll be there in some sort of rocking chair, counting the stars

Until you get there.

Poems

by Seth Kaye

still, ask for help

the people who used to check on me
aren't those people anymore
i drowned them all accidentally
and i don't even know what for

Photography by Brendan O'Donnell

remember to live

i do not think i will ever be so strong
as to not feel the passing of time
even the stoutest of hearts
are found embedded in aging forms
it's a raw circumstance and a labored rhythm that sustains life
purely by the force of misunderstood and misinterpreted mystery
... and some sort of chaotic cosmic order
what pattern was made present
that now keeps my breaths in line
following one after the other
while Distraction crowns himself my king
and means to render me without legacy
or poignancy
because if it were up to me
i would have forgotten to live long ago

a good book

i want to travel back
just a little while longer
tie my shoelaces to the last sentence
on every page
leave me here just one more moment
smelling like i've lived through
something brave and
the ink all over me has meaning
more than any explanation i can now give
forgive me for not wanting to live

but a good book ...
something i can retreat to
a channel of safety
where the riptide stops tearing at my legs
loosens its grip
and sends me up for air

----

there is a thread i cannot hold onto
something about life
so attainable for everyone
who doesn't think too much about it
but a lacerating wire
for those of us with tender palms
five fingers wrap around this thin line
five more more of the same
but my hands are made of light
reflected from some far off source
where my body is

THE MOURNING CIRCLE
BY BLAKE SLAUGHTER

Alexandria woke in the throes of confusion

---

unlike any she had ever felt before. A dense forest stood silently above her waking eyes and fallen leaves ensconced themselves in her tangled hair. She was undoubtedly in a place unfamiliar to her memory- which had almost entirely vanished. She could remember her full name: Alexandria Rose Bowen- Alex for short. She could also remember it had been warm before waking in this cold, damp place. However, the weather was of minor importance to her now that she found herself unguarded in a foreign land.

"Hello?" she spoke quietly to the endless congregation of trees.

No reply. Not even the faintest gust of air could be heard, which made her change in position from lying to standing sound like a dangerous inferno spreading through a remote village. Alexandria Bowen, possibly the last survivor of a major catastrophe, was alone in this world at last.

While the average human craved to be alone periodically, even Alex, occasional indulgence swiftly develops into terror when there is nowhere or no one to return to. Now the current question plaguing her was: *Who was out there?* or, more notably, *What was in here with her?*

"I'm armed," she lied. "I have a gun!"She heard a weak laugh in return. The sound seemed to come from behind her, where, upon turning, she could suddenly see a clearing in the trees and a tall figure that was undoubtedly human. Something felt horribly wrong- worse than it already had- and there was no way that the odds of this predicament were going to be in her favor. There had been no animals in her field of vision since she woke- just her, the forest, and the laughing figure in the distance. As she stuck her foot out in the direction of the unknown individual, the leaves crunched loudly, and a nameless gloom came down upon her. Alex briefly believed it to be the anxiety of oncoming death, but disregarded it and continued through the dense greenery with forced courage.

She could see the figure more clearly as they came into view and discovered it was not only human, but a young male. This boy, presumably a teenager, had long blonde hair streaked lightly with dirt and a face that was painted liberally with concern and a precocious demeanor. Nonetheless, through his obvious worry, he smiled at Alex, who had stopped in her tracks twenty feet from him. There was a girl- around the same age as the boy, she guessed- next to him. She had long hair, blacker than a total solar eclipse that contrasted her white dress. After a moment of hesitation, she entered the circle.

The boy, in a dark red suit, straightened his posture and prepared to greet his new guest, "Hello, I'm Ellis Maddox." He spoke with a disposition darker than the stories of bloodletting and ethereal apparitions that Alex read in the midst of her adolescence.

"Welcome to Purgatory."

Alex laughed nervously, "What?"

"My name is Ellis Maddox." he repeated, "Though you may call me *Mister* Maddox..."

"No, I heard exactly what you said," Alex interrupted, "But I was expecting a standard greeting and maybe an explanation as to why you and I are here together?"

Mr. Maddox placed a careful hand on the other girl's shoulder, "This is Emma." he continued, as if oblivious to Alex's question, "And you are?"

Surely this Maddox boy was suffering a delusion, and delusional boys were boys that you did not dare cross,

"Alexandria," she answered. Mr. Maddox extended his hand to shake hers, and the girl named Emma did the same. Alex immediately thought of lies she could tell to escape the clearing safely. In an unthinking manor, she patted the outside of her pockets. Mr. Maddox noticed this and smiled empathetically, "Our material belongings do not come with us, unfortunately."

This meant that Alex was without her phone and wallet; or more importantly, the numbers and money that came with them. There was an aching question plaguing the air now more than ever as she looked upon this young man's face, "How old are you?" she asked. Maddox chuckled and met her gaze, "I'm sixteen," he answered, "But I've been here for forty-five years."

Alex let out a brief, hysterical laugh. She knew that this was an obvious lie, but she couldn't let him know this, "How long have I been here?" She asked with forced interest in Mr. Maddox's delusional propaganda. To Alex's blatant surprise, the boy looked directly into the eyes of the sun and slowly followed the shadows it cast downwards into the woods, "Well, judging by the sun's movement, about two hours." This was complete and total insanity. Alex decided that it was time for her to leave, "I thank you both for your time. I really do. I respect whatever creed you uphold. However, I must be honest and say it isn't for me. May I go now?"

Maddox stared at her blankly, "You've always been free to go, Alexandria Rose. Though, I do feel compelled to warn you of the beasts beyond the circle. They have a rather indefatigable lust for blood." *The beasts* Alex thought despairingly. Were these creatures quite literally animals or Mr. Maddox's guards of this small forest clearing? She instantly thought of an army of mutated congregation members emerging from behind the trees beyond and chasing her through the woods; members that outnumbered her; who were stronger and more powerful than her; who actually believed in the dogma of these two people lost in the woods. Was this what he meant by beasts and... *how did he know my middle name?*

"Did you steal my license while I was asleep?" she asked defensively.

"No." He answered, maintaining his blank expression, "As I stated previously, our belongings don't follow us."

"Then why did you ask my name if you already knew it?" Alex demanded.

"I haven't forgotten the ways of earth and its common courtesy culture." Ellis smiled charmingly, "I thought that addressing you by your middle name may call to mind a memory or familiar face."

It didn't. Alex felt nothing but an uncomfortable wave of oppression swallow her whole. This man owned her and he knew it. "You might as well remain here in the circle… at least for now. The sun is setting quite rapidly." Distracted from the numerous questions she yearned to ask this strange boy, Alex pointed her vision upwards to the previously blue sky to see a blood orange shade draped around her and the others. It was as if Edvard Munch himself had begun painting *The Scream* in the stratosphere above them.

Maybe it was that intimidating color in the sky, or maybe it was the uncomfortable silence that followed his invitation, or maybe it was that the girl named Emma had remained silent since Alex's arrival, letting only the boy speak, but something told her that maybe those mysterious beings beyond the outer limits of the circle weren't as dangerous as the ones beckoning her to spend the night with them. So, she turned and ran. She ran from the strangers and her likely death. She ran from the ominous shadows aided by the evening sky and the fear; that awful fear that wouldn't subside. What Alex desired now was total anonymity; a promise that the next person who found her would be previously uninformed of her existence and willing to help her.

Slowing down, she came upon copacetic piles of pine cones surrounding a dead tree, "Hello?" she called quietly, worried she would alert Maddox by yelling. She examined the tree, walking through the pinecones and closer to it. Though the sun was more limited here, she could make out a carving: the face of a woman. The woman was not only sorrowful, but screaming in agony. A new fear danced across the distant hinterland of Alex's mind; that she was in the domicile of the so-called beasts. Adding to her inauspicious sojourn in the woods, the orange tint of the sky had almost seamlessly transformed into a mournful royal blue, blocking a comprehensive view of her environment.

A small fragment of her wanted to stay in the dark, but Alex knew that that wasn't possible, so she resumed moving slowly. Something scraped her side, causing her to shriek in terror. The sound of pinecones tumbling to the ground behind brought relief. Though seconds after, she heard a crunch, causing her to violently turn and face her potential aggressor, "Mister Maddox?" There was someone or something standing in front of her that she couldn't see. It took another step in her direction, "I'll come back to the circle. I swear. Just lead me back."

There was a sharp breath before the shadowy humanoid figure spoke, "I can smell your fear."

Alex was rooted firmly into the ground, embodying the vegetation that encircled her. The breathing of it became louder and she could feel its lust for her. However, her longing for an escape was greater and she sprinted past it, finally freeing herself from terror. Sudden gusts of wind whipped at her unprotected face and arms, terrifying her to the point of hysterics as it sent weak branches off trees and into her path. Pleading and praying for help in her vast surroundings, she screamed desperately.

> **" Yet, at the climax of all this fear, there was the boy and the girl, and somehow Alex felt safer in the company of the strangers.**

The moon briefly allowed her a guiding light to see her stalker running alongside her ninety yards away, "It's going to kill me!"

Distracted by her pursuer, Alex fell over a tree root and landed on the ground. The smell of the damp leaves infiltrated her senses and told her to accept what was coming to her. *You can shut it out* they told her, *it'll be over before you know it.* The rapid footsteps dissolved into leisurely ones. *The monster would feed at last as it closes in on its victim* Alex thought dementedly, *I surrender.* A cold hand touched her shoulder followed by a jagged exhale, "Alex," the voice said, "Are you ready to listen now?"

Maddox extended a hand to Alex's muddy one and pull her from the ground. The moon cast its light more intensely here; illuminating the once beautiful blood orange canvas- now a wild jungle of killers brought about by nightfall. The fear that dawn would never surface on the horizon was affixed to the fear of murderous silhouettes in the confines of this outlandish place. Yet, at the climax of all this fear, there was the boy and the girl, and somehow Alex felt safer in the company of the strangers.

"If you still think I'm mad, consider me your deliverer from evil."

Maddox said, breaking the silence. Alex tried to recall memories of something; anything. "I don't think you're crazy," she said. She was lying, but what was the likelihood of her honesty being well received? Instead of developing an unwanted conversation, Alex struggled to vehemently generate mental images and attach them to genuine recollections. "They'll return to you in due course, Alexandria. The fond and the horrid recollections of the yesteryear and beyond will resurface with spontaneous might." he spoke calmly, beginning to whistle. The sound of it bordered the realm of things that weakened one's stability and those that pleased the senses- like Marilyn Monroe softly singing *Happy Birthday, Mr. President.*

"I remembered something." Alex said, stopping in her tracks just inside of the circle. She could see that Emma was sleeping on a decomposing log.

"What's that?" Maddox asked, ceasing his melody.

"Marilyn Monroe and J.F.K.

"That's good." He said, pursing his lips, "But I dare you to find valor in the face of perplexity. Search from within, Alexandria."

It was as if this command had brought about psychological anarchy by refusing to obey the wall erected to control her thoughts and at last overthrew the venomous governor: her own mind. The barrier had not been completely demolished by the mad mental mob just yet, but it was penetrated enough for Alex examine the grounds on the other side of it. Through these crude windows shone spotlights, revealing convoluted memories. The celluloid images danced on perennially without a known principle. A fire grew internally and started to burn those images, allowing the smoke to cloud her brain and cause pain.

"I can't!" Alex howled in anguish, waking Emma from her seemingly tranquil slumber. Mr. Maddox appeared to be saddened by this outcome, but assured her that her failure was perfectly normal. "It took me some time too," Emma spoke. Alex, who was beginning to think this poor girl was eternally mute, was stunned by the girl's sudden entry into the conversation. Maddox was delighted and encouraged Emma to tell the story of her former life. Emma smiled slightly as she sat up on a log.

The story began with an illustration of a resplendent Sunday in a suburb outside of Seattle, Washington. She spoke of the nature of her home state and its political progressiveness as she beamed with pride. However, the artistically attractive landscape of ecstasy was soon slashed to reveal a portrait of savagely dark happenings hidden behind it. "My father wasn't well," she told them, "He had told me this two months prior and to keep it secret." she began to weep softly, wiping her tears with her bare hands. Maddox stood firm, but frowned slightly. "I wanted to surprise him; make him feel like he was normal. He was my father and I loved him." she stumbled on her words, gasping for air, "But he took my life that day. I've been trying to forgive him from the moment he pushed me, but I don't know if I can."

Mr. Maddox sat beside Emma and took her head calmly into his arms as she wept incessantly. With the conclusion to an unspeakably violent narrative, Alex accepted this current state of affairs as reality, rather than a horrible nightmare. However, she was still very much alive when compared to these individuals; who were unquestionably ghosts. Rather than proclaim her newfound revelation to the preoccupied pair, she lay down on the log across from theirs and observed them. Something in the way he held her was inhuman, yet not precisely supernatural either. He clasped her so fiercely, yet so emotionlessly; like a naïve child unaware his mother had been sentenced to death by hanging.

A slight wind crept through the trees and up her skin, delivering the reassurance of safety in a time of enigmatical happenings and sending her into slumber. Here, the sound of classical music was presented gradually; first as subtle as a single bee in a field of lavender, then as loud as the sounds heard from a city sidewalk. Her own personal orchestra serenaded her to the visual delights of the things she thought she'd never see again: an open plane outstretched over the horizon, families, couples, laughing children. She danced enthusiastically to the violins as those couples and families encouraged her. The children playing in the nearby fountain ceased their splashing and joined her at once.

There were laughs all around, but not mocking ones, ones associated with permanent confidants and familiar security. The music began to die, causing her to open her eyes to the continual lawn once again. Everyone had stopped dancing, yet their smiles were still etched on their faces. To her left, a woman still had her leg in the air and her hands outstretched to the sky. Alex blinked. So did the woman. "Alright," Alex said aloud, "This isn't real. You're going to wake up in the circle again. It won't be optimal, but it'll be real."

"You don't know what *real* is anymore." the woman said. Her mouth hadn't moved when she said this, but Alex knew it was her. The music began once more, but its noise was chaotic. The trumpets become the prominent forefront of the band as the people moved to dance around the fountain as it went from a stream of crystal blue water to a gushing dark red liquid. In the fountain, she could see a car overturned next to her own body, which was draped backwards over the ledge; eyes bulging and an open mouth that silently screamed *help me.*

Emerging from the nightmare and back into reality- or something like it- Alex was greeted by Mr. Maddox, who sat in the same place as the night before. Something was strange in his demeanor. He wasn't sorrowful, but he wasn't exuding felicity either. Nevertheless, he did give the impression of being somewhat pleased, "What did you dream of last night?" he asked. Alex needn't explore her mind for the illustrations, she could recall every detail vividly, "I dreamt I was dead." She said bluntly, not wanting to discuss the subject further.

"Well, that's because you are."

Trying to ignore his sarcastic remark, Alex sat up and noticed something missing, "Where did Emma go?" she asked. Maddox shrugged his shoulders nonchalantly, "She probably walked the marble staircase or something. It's best not to become committed around here." His voice was grave now and his eyes refused to meet her. "You killed her," Alex accused him.

"Killed her with what, Alexandria? A loose twig? You're being juvenile." He stood, towering over her sitting body even from ten feet away, "I think I'd dare to say you're manufacturing a pipedream because you can't accept your own death."

"No." Alex protested.

"Come on, Alexandria Rose. You remember."

And the truth was, she did. It couldn't be true, but those thoughts were there oppressing her and sending her into denial and madness. "You overindulged in those worldly drinks at one of your friend's untamed gatherings because you were feeling a bit burdened that day." He began.

"No!" Alex spat through clenched teeth.

"Rather than tolerate that awful shame a moment longer, you drove away at once. Now, you were driving moderately fast and you hardly saw the other car on the dark road. Poor thing; she was only seventeen." Alex tried her hardest to identify these explanations as untrue, but couldn't bring herself to do so over the roaring guilt in her heart and soul- that was, if she still possessed either. "And rather than report the incident to the authorities, you ran, like you did yesterday when you arrived; like you always do. But your story doesn't end there. You drove further down that dark road and you stopped for some shuteye, assuming it was all a hallucination from whatever was in that powerful punch, but oh no. See, you hadn't known that the front page of the local newspaper boasted a killer that had been making the rounds because you had been so shallow up until the moment that he arrived at your car window."

After explaining, he walked closer to her, further intensifying Alexandria's unease and puzzlement, "That dream you had showed you what should've happened that night."

She mustered up the courage to respond with what she had been yearning to ask him from the very moment they locked eyes, "What are you?"

"I'm Ellis Maddox," he said, "And *you*, Alexandria, need to repent for your wrongdoings."

He reached for her hand, but she found herself running again- like she always does. Sprinting at a speed she wouldn't have thought imaginable. She watched the contents of the woods pass by in a green blur. "Alex!" he called for her. She didn't turn back, but something stopped her in her tracks. She was in the lair of the monster once more, only daylight remained firmly by her this time, exposing a decomposing mannequin under the shade of a tree. At its feet was a large speaker which said those chilling words when Alex was within six feet of it: *I can smell your fear.* Soon after, Ellis' beckoning came as a warning of his proximity.

What is this place? she thought helplessly to herself.

Whatever this hermetically sealed dwelling was, Alex wanted out of it, and that's what she was going to get. She left the lair and continued forward, jogging to save energy, and soon found a hill where the shade of the green was scarce and a road shared its peak. Maddox called to her as she flagged down a car passing by. "Alex, no!" The driver manually unlocked his passenger side door and pushed it open for her. She stepped in, telling the man to drive as Ellis materialized, banging on the windows. "Are you ok?" he asked. Alex told him she wasn't. "Alright, the police station is just up the road."

"No!" she shouted, "I just want to get out of here."

"Alright," said the man turning to her, "I know where we can go."

The door locked with the click of a button and he stared back into her eyes. The coldness; that lifelessness that'd been clarified by the moon that night was now being seen in the daylight. As they neared a mountain tunnel, a domineering warmth loomed over both of them. She cried regretfully.

LESS BROKEN

BY LONDYN RAYNE

I'M COMFORTED

WHEN YOU CRY WITH ME

THE COCKTAIL OF TEARS

IS A REMEDY

TO FEEL LESS

BROKEN

LET'S BE LONELY

COLLECTIVELY

MAYBE OUR SHARP CREASES

ARE ACTUALLY

PUZZLE PIECES

THAT FIT IN EACH OTHER'S

PICTURES

IN A CROWD

BY ZARAH GATES

In a crowd
Hundreds of people walk by
Each one with a name
A family
A signature dance
Some people like to hide themselves away
But what do you do when an extrovert becomes a hermit?
Notice me, I breath.

I don't just make coffee
"Is that for here or to go?"
"Is that for here or to go?"
"Is that for here or to go?"
"Is that for here or to go?"

I'm doing just fine today
Plastic kills turtles, but yes, you can have an extra straw.
No we don't sell soup
The bathroom is up the elevator, 2nd floor and to the right.
We're only to-go right now, is that okay?

Notice me, You're looking at a person, not a robot
"Is that for here or to go?"
It's easier to be deaf, to hide away
To act like you're pulse doesn't even work.
With every sip, I swallow more of my soul
That screams out
YOU'RE HUMAN
My tears on break are real.
It's just a rough season.
A life that goes completely unnoticed
HAVE A GOOD ONE!
Cup after cup after cup.
longing for someone to reach through the counter barrier
To feel my soul move

But that won't happen,
I'm just a face
In a crowd

NOCTURNA

BY DARRYL PICKETT

Nocturna leapt from the open window

---

of the bedroom, out onto the grass below. She landed effortlessly on four paws, then ran the perimeter of the house, staying close to the lattice skirting at its base. At the back porch, she reached the broken panel that provided entry to the foundation beneath the abode. There she often found live prey to supplement the pureed, flavorless meats given to her twice daily by her hosts. Tonight she found nothing, save the bones of a young grackle she had eaten days before.

There would be plenty of hunting at the abandoned yard. And she ached for a good hunt. But she felt a pang of unease when she turned her gaze that direction. Five nights ago, she had followed a lost brown rabbit into the tall grass of that lot. An unusual scent had met her nostrils, a scent not just unfamiliar, but threatening, as well. It had reminded her of the smell of dead things that had gone uneaten for too long. But rotting meat was a passive smell, unpleasant but stagnant. This smell had seemed active, alive. It had made her black fur prickle.She slinked to the front yard, and there she found Patter, the young tortoiseshell from the corner. Patter was her favorite of the neighborhood cats. She approached, and they smelled and greeted each other.

Patter was on her way to the overgrown yard. Nocturna lowered her ears and growled.

"There's something not right there. A bad smell."

"I know." Patter followed her own tail in a half circle, then sat down on the soft cut grass of Nocturna's home. "It's gone now. Chaser said it's all right to hunt there tonight."

"I haven't seen Chaser around much lately."

Not that it bothered her. Chaser had sired her first and only litter three years earlier. Since that time, her hosts had taken her for the procedure, the strange dream after which she was no longer fertile, and so not useful to Chaser, who sought to propagate as often as possible. He still treated her as if she ought to be submissive in his presence. She enjoyed defying this expectation.

"He asked about you last night." Patter began grooming her left flank,

"What reason would he have to ask after me?"

"He didn't tell. But you should come with me. He's certain to be there."

"If he needs to know of me, let him come to my window and deal with me there."

"Branches will be there."

Nocturna looked at the old house at the end of the cul-de-sac. "Why would Branches gather at that yard. He doesn't hunt."

"Maybe he just likes the company."

"Very well. I would like to see Branches again."

Branches was the only kitten from her litter who had remained in the neighborhood. He was spoiled and pandered to by his hosts. But she enjoyed his playful spirit.

Nocturna followed Patter down the street, around the again, unoccupied house, and into the yard. She spotted prey in the brambles of the old flower bed, and without a thought, she pounced. In seconds, she had a field mouse trapped beneath her claws, and her teeth clenched in a fatal bite around the back of its neck.

"I didn't even see that!" Patter gazed admiringly at her catch.

Nocturna recognized a hunger in Patter's eyes. "Have your hosts not fed you?"

"Not for days. They left. Got in their machine and left. They aren't the only ones."

Nocturna dropped the dead mouth and nudged it toward her.

"Take this. I'm still well fed."

Patter accepted the gift, jumped onto it with sudden voracity.

When she was done, the two crept through the tall grass, toward the clearing near the broken fence.

They found Chaser sitting on the tree stump, a frequent nighttime perch. His orange and brown stripes stood out in the moonlight, glowing nearly as intensely as his eyes.

"So Nocturna has come at last. Thank you for bringing her, Patter"

He hopped off of his perch and rubbed his flank up against Nocturna, purring deeply as he did so. She lowered her ears and hissed.

"What's wrong, Nocturna? It's not as if we don't know each other."

She sensed something off about him. Something directly related to the strange scent. That was gone, but the animated, uneasy electricity clung to him, made him repulsive.

"Keep a distance, Chaser."

"If you prefer." He approached Patter instead, and licked the back of her neck. "Patter doesn't mind my attentions."

Nocturna growled. "Patter seeks to have a litter. I think she could find a better mate."

"Perhaps." He pulled away from the young cat. "I have something to ask you."

Nocturna faced him, keeping her defensive posture. "What is it?"

"Your hosts, they have a spawn, an infant."

"That's right. For months now."

"There is a rumor that you like this naked, pink monster. I've even heard that your hosts allow you to sleep with the awful thing."

"They trust me. And yes, the little one likes the warmth of my body, and the comfort of my purring."

Chaser made a throaty, hawking sound. "And I thought Patter had been over-corrupted by her hosts. Here you are trying to make yourself mother to one of their squalling blobs."

"What is it to you!"

"I want to see this infant."

Her entire body went tense at this suggestion. She arched her back and raised her hackles.

'I see you object. I thought you might."

"I'd like to see Branches. Otherwise, I think I'm done with the yard tonight."

"Patter and I are waiting for Branches. He'll be here soon. You see, Patter intends to mate with our son."

'You know that's not possible."

"Isn't it?"

"His hosts took him to the cold place, and ended his ability to mate. Just as my hosts did to me."

"Yes. That's true. I don't know how you abide by them after such cruelty. But Branches has been restored."

"Restored how?"

"I know you've felt it in the air. A powerful change. Branches is complete again. Ready to mate and hunt."

"I want to see him." Nocturna felt her spine shake and tremble as if lightning were gathering within it. The dread kept her fixed on the spot, staring at Chaser even as she tried to adopt a warning posture.

"I think he is ready to emerge," Chaser warned. He rocked back on his hind haunches, and his body twitched. His abdomen bulged and twisted. His mouth stretched into a yowl of agony and anger.

His belly split open, and out of it tumbled a mottled pouch of bristling for and muscle. It pulsed and grew, and soon, took on the recognizable form of Branches.

Chaser and the newly emerged Branches rolled to one side, conjoined at the center, appearing to wrestle one another, until Branches broke off of the other cat and wobbled to his feet. Within a matter of terrible seconds, he puffed up, his bones snapping and reforming, his muscles expanding, flexing. Finally, he stood on all four paws, proud and ferocious, and beautiful.

Chaser, at the same time, and re-formed and revitalized from the violent transformation. Both cats turned their gazes on Nocturna. Branches addressed her.

"Hello, mother. It's good to see you."

"Branches! What's happened to you?"

Branches leapt to her and butted his head against hers. "I've been reborn, mother. Many times, and I get stronger with each rebirth. I'm whole again, and ready to make more like me."

Nocturna sprang back and ran to Patter's side.

"This isn't right!"

"It's not about right or wrong. It's about strength and power. We have returned to our true, original nature. Ferocious, brutal. Haven't you noticed? It's been in the air. Our captors, those clumsy two-legged hosts, they are afraid of us. They are running away. Even Patter. Her hosts fled in terror when I entered their home. Isn't that right, Patter?"

Patter licked Nocturna behind the ear and purred lightly. "It's true, Nocturna. Branches came to claim me as his mate. When he first attacked and abosorbed me, they saw. And they were so frightened, they got into their rolling machine and left."

Nocturna stepped away from Patter, "He absorbed you?"

"Yes. We can join together and we can separate, as you have seen. One of us can contain an army. And our brood will be born with the same power."

Patter rolled onto her back, and Branches grasped her tail in his teetch, She lifewise bit into his rear haunches, and then, as one, they rolled and mutated together, stretching and shrinking, rolling around in a ghastly ball until they were one, wearing the appearance of Branches.

"Isn't it amazing, mother?"

Nocturna finally found the strength to move, to run. She tore away from the little clearing and sprinted away, through the tall grasses, the ruined garden, and around the side of the abandoned house.

Chaser caught up with her, got directly in front of her and pounced, pinning her to the ground.

She swiped him with her small, razor-sharp claws. She drew blood as she slashed across his face. He bit her neck, forced her into a roll, and dug his own much larger claws into her side.

Then he released her.

"I won't take you yet. I want to get to the baby. I want you to lead me to it. Let me alone with it."

> **❝ She felt the electricity glow within her. The places where her wounds had healed began to quiver.**

She took one more leap at him. She dug the claws of her front right paw into his left eye, piercing it. He let out a yowl of pain.

Then she ran, a blur of black fur in the darkness of night, until she was in her own yard, beneath the window of the room where the hosts kept their infant. The window was no longer open.

She meowed and cried. Not long after, the front door of the house opened.

The female two-legs host saw her and called out the sounds that Nocturna had learned, over time, were meant to summon her. She darted into the house.

The female host picker her up, and her face betrayed fear and alarm. She gently held Nocturna and ran hands and fingers lightly over the places where Chaser had injured her.

Soon, Nocturna was in the water room, being held near the basin from which water flowed, being wiped down with squares of woven cloth. She could see her own blood being absorbed by the soft panels. But her host looked less worried. The hands poked and pulled at her fur, looking for wounds.

Nocturna was soon aware that, in spite of the blood, there were no injuries, no cuts. She felt a warm, vibrating sensation that she soon realized was her own purring. At the places where Chaser had bit and scratched her, she felt unusual sensations of skin and muscle regenerating and strengthening.

The host, the mother of the infant, continued to wash her fur, offering loving strokes and scratches behind her ears. The father host soon appeared. His face, usually happy to see Nocturna, showed only worry and fear this time. His voice sounded tense and urgent.

"He knows," Nocturna thought to herself. "He knows about this unnatural brood of cats. He thinks I may be one of them."

She turned to the father host with large eyes, tilted her head and gave a sweet, high-pitched mew, as if to reassure him that she was all right.

She was set onto the floor, and the two hosts went down the corridor and into their own chamber, where they continued to make agitated noises toward one another. Nocturna saw that boxes and blankets had been set just inside the front door. She knew the signals that the hosts were about to load things into the great rolling machine outside.

Nocturna remembered the awful goal that Chaser had told her about, his desire to visit the infant. She ran straight into the room where the little one slept inside of its raised bed surounded by wooden rails and bars. With one practiced jump, she was next to the baby, wrapping herself nose to tail next to it, and purring comfort and safety.

The little one cooed a happy sound at Nocturna's arrival. She stayed stil, curled and purring, until the infant slept. Down the hall, the noises of argument and activity continued.

"All is well," Nocturna told herself. "I can stay with this helpless being and offer my protection from Chaser, and the others. They are no longer my kind. They are not cats. They have become something else. And I will fight them if I must."

The noises died from within the house abated, and there followed a few moments of quiet.

Then Chaser appeared at the nearby window, with Branches sitting to one side of him, and Patter at the other. They stared at the little one. Chaser placed his paws on the clear glass and raised himself onto his hind legs. He seemed to grow taller as he did so.

She felt the electricity glow within her. The places where her wounds had healed began to quiver. Her flesh and fur twitched.

She had been infected. She would change. She would become like those others. And if that happened, she would harm the infant.

Her purring had stopped. And the absence of that purring woke the baby, and it began to cry.

The mother host appeared, and began making the familiar noises of comforting and care to her own child. Then she noticed Nocturna.

She lifted Nocturna and carried her out of the room. Then, Nocturna saw that she was being lowered into a familar container, the hard box with the wire door. This ritual always occurred just before they placed her into the rolling machine and took her away from the house. Often it was to visit the cold place, where she had undergone the cuts and changes to her body. The alterations that made it impossible for her to bear any more kittens.

But just as she thought about this, as the wire door was shut and the box set next to the front door, Nocturna felt the lower part of her body pulse and swell with warmth. She looked toward her lower belly, and saw the transformations taking place beneath her skin. She was being restored. Just as Branches had been.

The injuries that Chaser inflicted on her had done this, had infected her blood with these alien powers of regeneration. The changes were happening quickly.

In her mind, new thoughts began to intrude on the old. Her feelings of affection and gratitude for her host family were pushed aside by jolts of resentment, waves of contempt.

"They are the enemy," she thought. And instantly, she fought off the new instinct and tried to focus on he rmemories of comfort and contentment.

Because the new thoughts were dangerous. Especially to the infant.

And she loved the little one. Her instinct to protect that defenseless creature asserted itself above the terrifying new impulses.

But for how long?

If she and the baby remained together, and if the changes grew stronger, then Chaser might easily win. She needed to get as far away as she could, as quickly as possible.

She needed their attention. She yowled, loud and furious.

The two hosts ran into the room almost immediatetely, and looked at her in shock.

She increased the intensity of her cries, and in doing so, felt a surge of strength and vehement power through her entire body.

She felt a pulse of energy as her limbs stretched and twisted. Her body shook and grew. Within seconds, she was too large for the hard little box she had been shoved into. And it made her angry.

She closed her eyes and pressed her will against the confinement that surrounded her.

And she felt a swell of triumph as she felt the box buckle and burst away as she grew and swelled further.

The mother host was terrified, crying. Then she turned and ran down the hall, to the room where the little one slept.

Nocturna, now three times her previous size, muscular and covered in wire-thick black fur, ran down the same hall, got past the mother host, then turned and confronted her, growling and baring her teeth, barring entry to the room by placing herself in the doorway.

"They are the enemy!" It was so clear to her now. They were her captors, beings who had ruined her body and softened her will, turning her from predator into powerless possesion.

And they would surely take the little one away in the machine. Take her away forever. Nocturna would not have it. The child was hers!

She turned to the baby's sleeping cage and stood on hind legs, placing her front paws on the rails and looking down at its sweet face, it's plump, wriggling body.

She jumped into the bed, her body almost instantly shrinking and collapsing, curling into its familiar sleeping postion.

She purred again, and easily found her old mind. She loved this tiny beast. She would give anything to protect it, to stay with it.

The mother host stood above her, face wet with tears, voice trembling. The mother host took her own infant into her arms, looking at Nocturna with a keening terror she had never before displayed.

Nocturna tried to allay her fear, mewing sweetly and rolling back to show her soft belly.

"It's going to be all right," she thought. But then the mother darted away into the hallway, and the feelings of tenderness turned to anger again. And her body responded by once again swelling and growing.

She prepared to leap out after her, but the father host appeared in the doorway, holding a tool with a long metal tube, pointed her direction.

A loud blast sounded, and a flash from the end of the metal pipe. Nocturna flet something blaze across the top of her head. The window behind the crib shattered. The host disappeared.

Nocturna turned to the broken window, and took a few moments to let her upper skull vibrate and strengthen. Then she leapt through the opening, scraping her rear haunches on the remaining shards of glass, hardly feeling it.

Outside, the hosts quickly threw boxes and bundles into the wheeled machine. They climbed into is and soon, it roared and rumbled to life and rolled away, squealing against the street as it rounded the corner and vanished into the night.

Nocturna felt a wave of relief. The infant she loved would be safe with them. Her relief became sorrrow. She sat on the lawn and lowered her head, licking her paws. They were healing. But she noticed that she was now, once again, her normal size.

Chaser, Branches and Patter strolled onto the sidewalk and sat facing her.

"We could have stopped them," Chaser said. "I could have taken the little one. I wanted to."

"Why didn't you?"

"Because your connection to it was too strong. You would have fought me, and your resistance would have forced me to kill you. So, I let them go."

She turned her head up and noticed the moon emergin from behind a dark cloud. Then she looked back at Chaser.

"Thank you for that."

And a few moments later, she felt the lingering stands of affection and sweetness dissipate, and the powerful waves of ferocious instinct asserted themselves, not just in her mind, but in her gut.

She stepped toward the other three and under the moonlight, she merged with them.

AUTHOR FOCUS
WITH DARRYL PICKETT

Darryl Pickett is a consummate storyteller and, as such, his creations fit naturally within these pages. In addition to writing stories, he also enjoys expressing his creative nature as an actor, playwright, and creative consultant for the theme park industry. He is currently working on his second novel, *Shark City Bay*, a crime story mostly taking place on Martha's Vineyard in 1974, during the summer when the movie *JAWS* was shot, which has a planned release of Summer 2020.

What has been your experience been as a creative writer in Florida?
I'm a native of New Mexico, though I lived in Maitland for a couple of years as a young child (around the same time Walt Disney World opened). I returned here thirty years ago to see if I could find creative work with Disney. In those three decades, I'd say Florida has provided more grist for the creative mill than I will be able to get to in this lifetime.

You were a staff writer for Disney at one time, yes?
Yes, and I still consult for them from time to time, and for the rest of the theme park industry. Being a creative writer for theme parks has no doubt informed some of my works, both in ways that embrace their energy and in ways that resist their superficial nature.

Theme park storytelling is immersive and fun, but it has thematic limitations. I get many more story ideas from the real Florida that lies at the fringes of that industry, or further out in its historic backwoods.

Does living in Florida inform your style in any way?
I've written a number of stories that take place in Florida, in different eras. The Girl On The Roof is the only one to have seen publication so far. But there's more on its way from that hopper.

(Continued on next page)

Does your work in theater inform your writing, and/ or the other way around?

They are both forms of storytelling I happily throw myself into. I write plays, and songs for musical theater, I write stories and novels as a literary pursuit. Any story idea I have, I ask myself if it will be best expressed on a stage, or on the page, in song, or some other form. The scariest ideas are the ones that feel like they should be cinema. I don't have the resources to make that happen yet!

Your lead story in this issue is about Christmas, and so is your first novel.

The novel came about after I spent several seasons wearing the big red coat and hat for a local tourist attraction. I got to see the world through the eyes of the iconic gift-giver, and that gave me a story idea. The result is *The Secret Feast of Father Christmas*, which I am relaunching soon as an audiobook.

You seem to be taken by the holiday itself, and the celebration surrounding it. Talk a bit about your relationship to Christmas, and the feelings it imparts to you and others.

Christmas is loaded with memories and emotional associations, both happy and melancholy. I know a number of my works come out of wanting to reconnect with the person I used to be; happy, naive, trusting, certain that the world was overflowing with good will. There is an inherent tension in writing about that youthful outlook, while carrying the weight of everything one has learned since, about the world and about oneself. Christmas is beautiful, evocative, and fraught with potential for sadness. That's quite a rich soil for growing a story.

CHRISTMAS WITH JERRY
BY AARON MORRISON

Jerry arranged the decorations just so

A cherished mix of family ornaments and nicknacks and adornments he had collected over the years. Snowglobes and tin soldiers on the mantel. Garland and a nutcracker on the end table. A motorized Santa, who had long lost his naughty or nice list, in the corner. His eyes lit up and a smile of childlike wonder appeared on his face as he switched on the toy train and it began its cycle around the christmas tree. Dozens of other ornaments, decorations, and trinkets looked on as Jerry almost skipped over to his keyboards. He preferred an actual organ, but that was too impractical. Jerry had worked the dual keyboard setup just as well. The extra control over the sound, as well as the portability, had appealed to Jerry. Though it had meant purchasing stands, foot pedals, cables, amps, and the like, he had never regretted the decision.

Jerry had sat on the folding piano bench and adjusted his large, thick rimmed glasses. A man in his 50s, he still had a bit of a youthful appearance about him. He attributed his boyish looks to the "magic and love of Christmas." He was roughly six foot three and relatively athletic. His hairstyle and outfit had a more conservitive Liberace look about it, which was the intent. Jerry had admired Liberace's showmanship, though he never went as colorful and extravagant. The black, crushed velvet suit, and slightly frilly white shirt he was wearing, was about as wild as Jerry got. He had grown up watching all those old Christmas specials, and various performances from his mother's era, and had taken inspiration from Jerry Lewis, Bing Crosby, and the like. He had wanted to learn to play the organ at the age of six, and his mother had obliged. Jerry was a natural, and took to the instrument quickly. Over the years, he developed his own take on the performance styles of his idols. Sure, there wasn't much money in what he did, but it brought him joy, and Jerry figured that was enough.Jerry had finished adjusting nobs and settings on his keyboards, positioned himself comfortably, and began to play. *Rudolph, the Red Nosed Reindeer* flowed from the amplifier as Jerry's expert fingers danced over the keys. He swayed and danced in his seat, smiling. He added his own flourishes to the song liberally, preferring the jazzy, almost improvised, feel to music. He always liked to start off with something upbeat and fun, and this was a solid go to. He pictured Rudolph, and Donner, and Dasher, and all the rest, frolicking and dancing in the snow to his music. His grin had grown even wider at the thought. He played through the song, finishing with a flourish, and a happy, satisfied little shake of his upper body and head.

Jerry made a few adjustments on his keyboard, readied himself, and started into his rendition of *Frosty the Snowman*. Fun little offbeat riffs and pauses for the drum machine. Jerry swayed excitedly until, about halfway through the song, he got distracted, causing his usually sure fingers to miss, making an off key noise. Frustrated, he slammed his hand down on the keys, which caused an unpleasant squawk to emit from the amplifier. Jerry stopped the drum machine and looked over at what had distracted him.

In the corner of the room, the woman had started struggling again and had let out an unintended whimper. Her husband was still out cold from the injection of midazolam Jerry had given him. The two children had been easy to subdue. The family of four laid there, arms bound behind their backs, legs tied at the ankles, and gags in their mouths.

Jerry, quickly and aggressively, strode over to the woman and knelt down, his face mere inches away from hers.

"Stop. Please stop." Jerry's voice shook in anger and frustration.

The woman's breathing had become more panicked.

"Just stop and enjoy the music!" Pleading had turned to demanding. "I'm just trying to spread some goddamn Christmas cheer!" Jerry removed a syringe from the case and brought it towards the woman.

She shook her head, eyes wide.

"Are you going to settle down and enjoy the music?"

The woman nodded. Tears continued to drip down her face.

"Good." Jerry put the syringe away. "Santa will be here soon, and we need to be in the Christmas spirit!" His voice had switched back to his usual calm and happy sounding tone. Jerry patted the woman on the shoulder, tousled the hair of her son, and skipped back to the keyboards.

He started back where he left off with *Frosty*, all the while smiling and mugging for his audience. He played a few more upbeat tunes, before eventually moving into the slower, religious based Christmas songs. His practically somber approach to the slow songs was in stark contrast to the showy style of the upbeat ones. This went on for close to an hour, though Jerry did not concern himself with the time. At one point, Jerry had gone back over to the woman, removed her gag, and asked her if she and the kids wanted to sing.

"Please let us go," she pleaded. Her voice exhausted and terrified. "We won't say anything. Please. No. No!"

Jerry replaced the gag and sighed. He looked at the woman with disappointment and sadness on his face. Jerry paused for a moment and returned to the music.

Eventually, after *Sleigh Ride*, Jerry looked up and around at the ceiling excitedly, a smile on his face.

"Do you hear that? I think he's almost here!" He smiled and winked at his audience. *Here Comes Santa Claus* erupted from the amp, sounding as giddy and excited as Jerry was. He played through the entirety of the song and continued to play as he pressed a few buttons on the keyboard, and adjusted a few things on another device. The music looped as Jerry stood and clasped his hands together in exuberance. He smiled and left the room. The tune continued to repeat over and over. Jerry reentered the room, a Santa Claus costume over his black, crushed velvet suit, and white, fake beard over his face. Santa took a moment to appreciate all the decorations and music, before turning his attention to the family. With a sigh, he stepped towards them. The mechanical Santa moved its empty arms and watched on.

***

News outlets reported another in the series of what they had dubbed the "Saint Nick Killings." A family of four had been found in their home, dead, coal stuffed in the mouths and eyes of the victims, as was the signature of the apparent serial murderer. Leaked police reports stated that the home, like previous locations, had appeared clean and undisturbed, save for a conspicuous spot on the Christmas tree where an ornament appeared to be missing.

*inspired by RLM and BOTW

THE NEW HOUSE

BY JOSHUA MAHN

The house was great

Just a simple, one-story, blue home in the middle of town. It cost quite a bit more than other homes its size nearby, but as soon as I had seen it online, my choice was made. I was magnetized to it. I dreamt about it. This house was where I was supposed to be.
It wasn't very different than any of my other options. No older or newer, not much bigger or smaller. It just was.

"Come on, just check out the new place." I goaded. My buddy Cecil lived nearby, and I'd been working on convincing him to help me unpack. I didn't have a lot of possessions, and I moved what I had into the house pretty quickly. Even so, the work was strangely lonely. I'd moved in several days ago by now, but still felt like I hadn't explored everything the new place had to offer.

Cecil eventually agreed, knowing full well that I'd task him with figuring out where I should put most of my stuff. He was a much more logical thinker than myself in this way.

"Why not put all these holiday decorations in the crawlspace?" he had asked me. I hadn't even been aware that I had crawlspace here.

"You're sure I have that?" I hadn't noticed anything resembling an entrance to the attic in my several days here, nor in the times I'd inspected the house before signing to rent.

"Pretty damn sure, dummy." He led me out to my humid garage and addressed my attention to the ceiling where, surely enough, there was a small rectangle of particle board- sloppily painted and quite old.

"Well, I'll be." I muttered. I'd always had a poor memory, with entire chunks of time in my life having gone missing, or simply remaining blank, but this took the cake.

"Alright, you win." I admitted to Cecil. I set my phone to the side, stood on my tiptoes, and, with a small hop, grabbed hold of the rope hanging from the attic door and pulled it down. A rickety ladder extended partway with a groan, refusing to go the full distance to the floor. The smell of hot must and the sickly-sweet, rotting fruit smell of guano stabbed my nostrils.

"Okay, well, I'm gonna see how much space is up there." I told Cecil, beginning my ascent. "Don't let me get trapped up there!" I joked, though with a suspicious sensation that I was more afraid than I liked to admit.

He laughed, and I crawled my way up into the attic. Expecting to hear the door slam shut behind me, I immediately turned, not caring to examine anything before I reminded Cecil that I would kill him if he let it shut. Peering up, he promised me again that it would stay open, and so I turned, and took in the sights.

What I noticed first was that my attic was much, much taller than I thought it could have been. I could stand up tall, with no issues. I blinked several times, waiting for my eyes to adjust to the light, and, after I scrunched them up and rubbed them one last time, I opened my eyes, and beheld an impossibility.

My attic was well lit.
My attic was very, very large.
Instead of dusty rafters and stray insulation, I observed a long hallway. A rich crimson carpet with gold trim led the way, and edison light bulbs in polished brass cages swayed very gently and discordantly, despite the still air.

I was terrified.

"Cecil..." I called, and, on hearing no response, elected to return myself to the ground as quickly as I could. I turned to find the ladderway, and yet, it was gone.

Not only the ladder, but the entire hatch down had vanished. There was no hole in the floor. No light from below. No breeze. No doors or hatches or anything that should have been. I crawled in the remarkably soft carpet, and I clawed dumbly at the dark wood-paneled walls to no avail. I screamed for Cecil and pawed for my phone, but found no luck with either. I had not merely become stuck, I had become trapped.

I spun madly. I became deeply fearful and strangely sleepy.

I could easily see I was in the tail end of the hallway. The small space behind where I had inexplicably appeared was free from noteworthy features, and the path ahead seemed to stretch strangely for thousands of feet. I was compelled, nearly forced, to look ahead, into the strange horizon. Only the path forward could have any solution, any chance of waking from this dream or discerning this strange trap.

So I did what anyone would have done when they became trapped. I looked for an escape. An exit.

And I began walking.

My feet led me down the hall before my I could tell them no. Before long, (though I had no interest or capacity for the discernment of time.) I could see identical sets of doors, laid evenly at intervals. It was at this point that I accepted that any resemblance to what should have been expected, or even possible, in the architecture of my home had vanished entirely.

Hesitant, tentative, I approached the first tall, gently damaged door. My hand hovered over the victorian-fashioned knob, and I quivered with an unknown fear. It was a childish fear, of having absolutely nothing to do except for that which you didn't want to do.

I took a breath, and opened it.

I could see a small room. The walls were a faded and dusty chalkboard green, the floors were a dryrotted and fragile wood gone punky with years of damp. An eerie and orange late-evening light filled the space, and offered me a hazy look at what sat behind a table expectantly.

I hadn't ever met it before, and yet, its name filled my consciousness at once as a deep and repressed memory is pulled to the front of your reality at the worst time.

The Man in the Chainmail Mask.

It merely sat ramrod-still at its schoolteacher-desk. I could barely perceive eyes, piglike, glinting from beneath its iron veil.

I was paralyzed. I could not move. It did not move.

The time seemed to pass to the tick of a metronome, to the only noise outside my racing mind, though the source of the noise eluded me at first.

I waited for the creature to attack. To wake me from this strange nightmare- after all, nightmares end, and they always end when you die, right? There's an expiration date on them.

But the entity did not move. It didn't release me.
Instead, we simply watched each other.
The gentle tapping continued.
I looked at last.
The gentle tapping was the sound of its fingers on the desk.
The Man in the Chainmail Mask had the most horrible hands.

Unable to stop myself from staring, I saw that each and every finger was unsettlingly long and slender, perhaps nine or ten inches, with uncountable knuckles. This length would have been much longer, except each was tied in on itself into a knot near the tip, each digit flaillike and mangled.

It drew a deep, rattling, rusty breath, and I ran.

I sprinted out of the room with everything that I had. My adrenaline was flooding, my breathing shaky. I didn't understand anything, I couldn't understand anything. I shut the door behind me as soon as I was back in the hallway, still and luxurious, and my panicked mass slammed against the next door.

I scrambled clumsily for the knob, took hold of it, lost my grasp, took hold once more, and pushed myself in. I slammed this door, and cursed myself immediately after for not trying to sneak away. My shaking fingers found the deadbolt lock, and turned it.

 This was my sanctuary now. It had to be.

I pressed my ear to the door, listening, listening, for the sound of movement beyond. For the sound of a raspy breath. For the metronomic fingers. I heard nothing.

I drew a breath of relief, my limbs all warmed, and my core ice cold from the fright, and turned to look at this new and strange room.

I saw I was in a library. Dusty shelves carved of dark wood stood from the floor to the high, vaulted ceiling. Rows and rows of these shelves seemed to stretch in every direction, and, though this room was very dim, my eyes danced over to a grand, curving staircase to the right. It had a richly carved bannister, leading up to a second floor full of the same. My eyes turned then to the left, and I beheld an identical twin of staircase, like a set of wings, and as my sight trailed down the stairwell I saw He was on it- standing and watching me.

I turned to leave the room and the door through which I had entered had vanished entirely. A blank wall stood in its place, and I turned once more in dumb disbelief to observe the entity before me.

I wanted to shrink away, to wake up, to cry, to die, but all of those things were out of my power. I could only ask.

"What…" I began, my voice cracking, "Are you?"

The creature moved closer, though slowly. I could see it was wearing a strange outfit of black cloth, not dissimilar to a puritan's dress, though interspersed were strange pieces of patchwork, and of chestnut-colored boiled leather. It has a ludicrous white collar, almost a mockery of elizabethan design, though much more like a lily pad. On its strange head hung its mask of chainmail, with thin, inefficient slats where eyes ought to be. Gray, malformed, pointed ears emerged as a rat looks at you from behind your kitchen cupboard.

It stopped walking down the steps, and I understood it had heard me. Its head moved slightly, and I could just barely see by the movement of the chainmail, that it was working its jaw in the same way one moves a limb around after ages of inactivity.

With a panting, file-like sound, it spoke to me, very quietly, but as if from within my own head. In a strangely pitched, weak, high voice, it commanded as it extended its knotted fingers ambiguously, saintlike, to the entire room at once.

"Look."

Trembling, I obeyed.

I approached the nearest shelf, fully aware of my caged state, cowardly hoping to please the thing before me, and withdrew the first book I could grasp. I pulled it down and opened it up, and browsed the strange contents.

It was me.
That is to say, it had pictures of me.
Baby pictures. And earlier, too.

Paging through, I saw my sonogram. I saw my mother swaddling me. I saw nurses carrying me. I saw my father carrying me into our home. I saw myself in a crib, and I saw myself in a highchair.

I saw myself in a bedroom, and I saw the photographer's reflection in the mirror. It was the Man in the Chainmail Mask.

The smell of old plastic and dust was rich on my nose, the photo albums were clearly aged.

I flipped through page after page, being met only with infant pictures of myself, especially of note were a few I had never been shown before, and a few which could not be explained. One image seemed to be of my birth, yet I could see now His chainmail-clad face in among the nurses, looking, eagerly awaiting my arrival.

I set the book down, but the command ripped through my head again.

"Look! Look!"
The thing stayed put, but its raspy words rang again and again. It laughed, eagerly, snorting and wheezing.

I picked up the next book, and was jarred by illustrations penned by my own hand, then lost to the sands of time. Coloring pages from restaurants. Preschool attempts at cats. Self portraits. Shredded pictures, taped together. Things which should have died. Things which I had thrown away. Things I couldn't understand.

I set this book down, and turned my gaze once more to the entire library before me. Hundreds and hundreds of shelves were ahead, with hundreds and hundreds of books upon each and every one of them.

"Look!"

I ran. I combed aisle after aisle, to the furthest corner of the room from the Man. I chose a book at random, and saw myself playing a computer game at age 14, back turned to the camera. This I cast to the side as I drew another, and saw myself in the bathroom brushing my hair.

I tore book after book off the shelf, and saw homework assignments, and small notes to friends. I saw printed out notes from my phone, and lists of my favorite usernames online. I found albums in which I was not the focus of the picture, but where I was simply walking behind someone else's photo, and I saw drawings others have made of me. I saw text conversations I had sent to friends, and conversations among others where I was simply mentioned.

I began screaming at a certain point, though I'm not sure when- I only know that my throat was raw and hurt horribly. As I ran, the Man in the Mask followed, though always at a gentle distance. "Look!" he kept saying, "Look!"

And I saw a door.
I bolted through it, my bile rising, and slammed it shut, as if that could possibly make a difference by now. I was starting to understand, or perhaps was simply confused enough to accept, that nothing could truly help me.

I saw the next sets of doors, and knew I had to try.

I approached the next, hoping still that perhaps this way held the key out of my nightmare, and opened the door to see a classroom as before. Only now, The Man in the Chainmail Mask stood patiently near to a chalkboard, and he was drawing strange, unlikely shapes, and pointing patiently to them with his knotted hands. I saw myself, though much, much younger, perhaps six years old, but very much there in the room with us, pointing excitedly at the board. He- I- was seated at a school desk, and my lunchbox was open on it. I called to myself but received no response. I slammed the door on this hellish hallucination, and opened the next in my mad pursuit. This room held only the head of the Man in the Chainmail Mask, but he was so, so much larger than he ought to have been. As he panted his ragged breaths in the middle of the massive space, spiders, cockroaches, flies, wasps, mice, and salamanders squirmed into and out of his mask, crawling around the eye slits, between rungs, into and out of his exposed, goblinesque ears. I ran, I don't even know if I shut the door this time, I just ran.

Door after door, I fled.

I saw myself sitting upon a stone, nude, nearly my own current age, being painted in oils by a tender-seeming rendition of the Creature. It exuded a soft kindness in this room.

I saw myself as a child in a bathtub, bug-bitten, as the creature ladled water over my head.

I saw the creature watch me, napping on the couch.

I saw a room where He and I were both writing things upon the walls. He wrote things like "Loyalty." and, "Devotion." and, "Patience." in neat, ageless font, and I saw myself, perhaps sixteen, scrawling madly, tears

> **"I flung a door open, and saw at last a withered and decrepit figure which I knew to be myself.**

running down my face. "I forgive, I forget."

In another room I beheld him writing on the walls with greasy paint, his strange knotted fingers dragging splattered marks far wider than what should be.

"I am with you always," he wrote in a gold shimmering paint. "I am cousin to the Orang Minyak. Brother to Akhkhazu. Tulpa of Tulpas. King among Boggarts, I am a keeper and I am an observer."

My blood ran cold, I retched, and could not void myself. I fled, and saw rooms in which I was my own age, as in right now. I saw myself mere days ago moving in while the Man in the Chainmail Mask watched from the back of the van. I saw in another room myself at my next birthday. I saw myself with partners.

I ran and I ran and I ran, ignoring doors altogether until I could take it no more. I flung a door open, and saw at last a withered and decrepit figure which I knew to be myself. I was rotting on a sterile bed. My name was written on a yellow clipboard at the foot.

I was in a nursing home.
I wish I had been alone- God, how I wish I had been dying alone in there.

Sitting next to my frail form in an uncomfortable chair, shrouded with the smells of sick and sterile, the Man in the Chainmail mask had a horrible, mangled hand draped gently on my knee.

I was his forever.

I leaned against the wall, hyperventilating, screaming to my future self to let him go. To die. To truly let it be. Not to numb but to see, and to truly forget. I screamed and I screamed, yet my old self did not hear. Only the Man in the Chainmail Mask heard. And by the faint tinkling noise of the rings moving, I knew his face was splitting in an enormous grin.

"Mine." he croaked from everywhere at once.
He spoke more easily now, encouraged.
"I am your ashes and your shadows and your dust and your smoke. Beginning to end, and you shall have none other before me or after me."

I turned, weeping, deaf, scentless, senseless. My ears ringing so loudly I wanted to rot, and, expecting to see another mirrored door behind me, I was shocked to see a stairwell down.

Carved roughly around it, the impressions sloppily painted in contrast to the rich accomodations elsewhere, were my name, my date of birth, those of my parents, and those of their parents, spinning and fanning out in a strange fractal hallucination. There were a great many other things carved there- names in no way associated with my family tree. Places I'd never been. Dates far, far in the past. Dates in the nearer future. I did not try to understand, I flung myself down the hatch.

I was bleeding. My knees were skinned against the garage floor, and I had splinters in my palms. The door leading into the house was open, and I could see Cecil standing in my kitchen.

I patted myself, bleeding, disbelieving I was here, disbelieving I was now.

"-...Or just ignore my whole question." Cecil muttered to himself.

"Wh-what...?" I managed, unsure what question I was asking out of every possibility.

"I asked if you were okay." And then, as if I were dumb, he added, "You tripped."

"I..." I looked around myself. "How long ago?"

"Jesus man, did you hit your head? You tripped on your way to the garage like two seconds ago."

"Two... two seconds?"

"Maybe a minute, I don't know." He was sounding concerned. "Look, do you need water or something?"

I took a deep breath and looked around myself, getting my bearings once more. I stood up, slowly.
"Yes, maybe I... Maybe I hit my head, is all. Quite right. That makes sense." I smiled painfully, and noticed I was clutching something within my pocket, and sat on the nearest box- a large plastic bin, filled with holiday decorations. Cicadas screamed madly, their decade-slumber finished. I could hear cars drive by. I heard my pulse.

Cecil spoke again as if he were repeating himself and tired of it. "Like I said, buddy. There's no crawlspace out there." I looked lazily now to the flat, flush ceiling. I thought of moving again but immediately knew it would do no good.

"I don't know where you were trying to go." He laughed a little. "Just stack that stuff in the corner in a minute when you're feeling better. We'll find a better place for it later. I'm gonna go get you a drink."

"Yes," I mumbled, confused. "Thanks, Cecil."
I looked down into my hand, and saw that I was clutching a photograph.
It was crumpled, sweat stained, and aged.

I smoothed it out against my leg. It was a picture of a nursing home, with
a familiar old man on a bed, with a familiar yellow clipboard at its foot. A
familiar shadow stood just behind it. I began chuckling as I saw it, and I
rasped to the empty garage, "Look."

IN LOW MORNING LIGHT

BY LYDIA SILBERNAGEL

You woke up before your voice
did— rolled over in bed and began
to tell me— all in whispers
of the world you visited

in last night's dream—
of the misty wood all
mottled green and dripping
in distilled sun— humming

with the definite tongue
of the white-throated sparrow
sung in perfect fourths—
and staccato beat breaths.

I rest my cheek on my hand
while you whistle her song.

PHOTOGRAPHY BY BRENDAN O'DONNELL

Detective Wade Knight was sweating again

The glow of the computer screen was bright and paranoid. The denizens of that digital world spat out insults like machine gun fire: cunt and whore and every other slur in the book. It seemed any provocation could do it, drawing them like flies to corpse-meat. The words began to lose their meaning.

But he had to make himself known in the cyber-world.

One thread, finally, seemed to be heading in the direction he wanted. The original poster was asking if anyone knew about the underground cabal. The politicians were all there, the thread posited. They were there right now and they were pulling the strings. The Hollywood actors were there, too, because they had always been part of the big sham, the great lie of America.

Then, a few posts down, it descended into ravings about the plague of immigration, and any substance was lost. Yet another digital trash-heap among the giant dumpster-fire.

Wade blinked the sweat from his eyes. It seemed like the A/C was acting up again. He reached for the Coke can on his desk and took a sip. It was lukewarm now and the sugary liquid rattled off the innards of the tin can. He sat back in his chair and looked around. There was nobody else in the office now, the pale, thin light flickering on rows of empty desks and fast food wrappers in trash cans.

Everyone else got to go out and pound the pavement, feet on the ground, kissed by fresh air, while he was stuck in a box. Every night after work when he got back to his newly empty home, he'd been going for long walks in the woods, just to be away from the glowering white screens, to let his soul breathe.

"How is it going out there?" asked his commander, Roland Pettigrew. Pettigrew was rotund and hardened, face like craggy rock. "Have you found any trace of them at all?"

"Not really," Wade said, sitting in the chair before his boss. Behind him, he heard the fan whirring, the chirping of telephones and human voices speaking low and dutiful into them, like a musical backdrop all around them. "I mean, everyone's fucked up on there. None more than the other."

"Yeah, well, we can't arrest all of 'em," Pettigrew said, taking a swig of his morning tea, a recommendation from his doctor to help wean off sugary sodas.

"We could try," Wade said.

"Just keep looking. They're not Gods. I know you can find something on them. These threats, the mayor's on my ass about them, you know."

Wade had found some threads, buried deeper into sub-boards and more obscure sites, that seemed to be leading him the right way. Did he know, one article asked, that there was a secret network of cannibal pedophiles working to control the government? Did he know that the leaders of both political parties were conspiring in underground tunnel meeting rooms to orchestrate tragedies around the globe? They had been behind 9/11, behind several mass shootings.

Wade read all of this until his eyes glazed over. His brain hurt and his eyes physically ached. His back was even groaning now.

There was no mention or trace at all of the other man, the city police officer, Dallas Holder, who had gone missing. He had asked around to a few people in messages, but none of them knew the other's name. They were still all their internet handles, even in 2019: skeevyguy73. DarthSlayer. PlasticFace. CuntArmageddon. They didn't care that these juvenile handles were all they were known by. They spent whole days trading their theories and tips, strengthening their conviction that they knew what was really going on.

And also, still no sign of any action. None of the bomb threats he was looking for, nor plans to stockpile weapons, as he'd been told. Just words. Words upon words, corroding his spirit. He became very sad. This was what humanity had come to.

Roland was folding up his coat over his arm and walking out of his office. He cocked his eyebrow at Wade. "Thought you were gone," he said.

"Nope," Wade said. "Still here."

"Man," Roland said. "Go home. We're all starting to worry about you, you know."

"Well, you don't gotta do that," Wade said. "I'm fine, man."

Roland gave him a penetrating look, withering and paternal. "Are you, though?"

"I just got to go through another page or two," Wade said.

Roland didn't get it, Wade thought. He didn't understand Wade's sheer perfectionism. He had always prided himself on this, on the completion of a job. It was how he had risen this far. He wasn't about to let his personal troubles get in the way of his career.

It was three days posting under aliases and pretending to believe vigorously in their conspiracies, inquiring vaguely as to others who were "serious" about the movement, until a man contacted him through email. He said his name was Jim, and he was asking if Wade wanted to meet and discuss "some things" about the movement.

They met the same afternoon at a Panera Bread in the poor side of the city, almost underneath the highway overpass, grimy looking and faded. Inside was a collection of bored and underpaid workers leaning on counters, talking in dull, slow tones, as if speaking slower would make the day go by faster. There was a smell about the place that bothered Wade as he came in.

Wade had taken care to look the part of the scruffy no-job conspiracy nut, with his beard grown out and clothes bought cheap from a GoodWill; dirty jeans and a worn green hoodie.

Jim sat at a booth near the back of the place. He had sallow, sunless skin and a purple dyed Mohawk, and wore an old Black Flag shirt and loose khaki shorts and sandals. His eyes were what Wade recognized immediately: here was the paranoia and the distrust, embedded in him like DNA.

He shook Wade's hand as Wade sat down. "Good to meet you," he said.

"Likewise," Wade said. "So you're the guy in the know."

Jim chuckled, a dry hollow sound, like he wasn't used to doing it. "I guess so. I mean, I just don't want you falling into some misunderstanding. I'm connected with some good people here. People who know what's going on. There are a lot of jokers who're just asshats, pretenders, posers, you know."

"Right."

The waitress took their orders. She came back a few moments later with black coffees.

"The people I know, we're trying to build a real movement," Jim said, leaning in, his voice low. "It doesn't seem like it all the time, I know, but there are others like us out there, and we're organizing. And we won't stop this time, like all the other times."

Wade nodded. He had been practicing his facial expressions in the mirror, all wide-eyed and skeptical and a bit afraid, but not in a necessarily negative way. In a way that suggested he was ready.

"So what brought you here?" Jim asked. "How'd you, y'know, find out about us?"

Wade gulped a mouthful of coffee. Too hot, still; it burned his tongue slightly. He tried to meet the man's eyes best he could. "Just had enough of the bullshit, really. I'm tired of the mainstream media shoving its agenda down my throat. Tired of being told what to think. And a while ago I had a pretty bad break-up, and that was just the final straw. I figured it was time to go deep. And I just want to... fucking go in it because so few people really do, and I feel like the world's going to shit unless somebody does something."

"I get that," Jim said. "Had the same stuff happen to me with women before." He cracked a skeletal jackal-like grin. They were just two guys now, bonding over guy stuff. The way Wade wanted.

"Exactly," Wade said. "So you know."

"There are chicks in our group who ain't like that. Who're cool."

Wade nodded. "Good."

"The break up, that was what spurred you to us?"

"I just felt like I was never taken seriously," Wade said. "By her, or by anybody. Everyone always just saw me as a joke. Always looked past me."

Behind Jim's sallow, pointed face, there was something twitchy and edgy and burning. He said they would show everyone how serious they were. They would make everyone listen and then the world would be like a cocoon, velvetine and warm, for them, finally letting them in from the cold.

"Well," Wade said, calculating his words. "How do you mean, that they'll see? Is there like, a plan?"

"It's forming as we speak," Jim said. "I can't say too much yet. Can't spoil the thing, but man, it's gonna rock your ass off."

Jim's Twitter feed was all links to various blogs with featured pictures of UFOs and Illuminati pyramid-eyes. There was a sizable amount of white nationalist rhetoric. All stuff gleaned from the same books and the same speeches: they wouldn't replace us, the immigrants were cross-polluting the country, separate but equal. It was, down to the letter, a cliché. Wade thought it shouldn't be so hard to have an original thought.

Jim texted him links to further reading material, telling him it was integral to the movement. Some of it was tinged with more anti-immigrant stuff, but most of it actually about the secret radio devices embedded in the skin of those who went to the ER. The radio devices heard everything, all peoples' conversations and private moments, and they were used for who knows what?

"It's all about the drugs," Jim texted. "They want to get everyone on drugs so we don't question them. Some kinda drug. Whether it's the opioids or the non-stop TV news. It's all drugs. Check what's in your food."

Roland Pettigrew told Wade he could see heavy bags under his eyes.

"It's good," Roland said. "Gives you more of a convincing look for this."

"Thanks," Wade said, feeling ants under his skin, and his eyelids like flimsy paper, itchy and brittle.

"Well, listen," Roland said, leaning forward, arm on his knee and a fatherly pitying look in his eyes. "We've arrested a few hoodlums, in the threats made recently. It was just a few jackasses. Some idiot kids who'll be going to the slammer for a few of their best years, now."

Wade felt hollowed out then. He recalled Jim with his snakelike eyes. "All due respect, sir, I think there's more here. I've been talking to some guys..."

He trailed off as Roland stared at him with blank, confused eyes. Roland said, "Well, sure, I mean, we don't aim to discourage any leads here."

Wade felt like he was being patronized. He just nodded and swallowed the acidic comments forming in his brain: this fat fuck, this hypocrite, he doesn't respect me even a little bit.

He was driving back home and felt his eyelids getting heavy. He was going 65 miles per hour on a rural road and his whole body became numb and floaty and his limbs weren't coordinating with each other. The car drifted off the road, wheels against uneven grass and soil. His eyes bolted wide open at the right time and he put a foot on the break.

As he jerked his car to a panicked stop, Wade felt something intensely, and he couldn't breathe. Everything was closing in on him unless he did this one thing, and he was pulling out his phone and dialing her number, the number that had been etched into memory even in these times where you didn't need to do that anymore, and the phone rang.

Lorelai picked up, voice melodious as usual, even in her disinterest. She could never control how her voice sounded like a songbird's chirping and it had annoyed her when he pointed it out, told her her voice was cute. "Wade?"

"Yeah, yeah," he said, trying to sound even, but the trembling was obvious in his voice.

"What is it?"

"Well, I was hoping we could… you see, I'm just on this dangerous thing…" He cursed himself for his dry mouth, his incoherence, nervous like a schoolboy. He must've sounded so dumb. He let the silence go too long, and she finally spoke up.

"Listen, I have to get out of here soon," she said. "I've got an appointment. Maybe we can talk later."

But her tone said what her words would not.

The next day he met Jim at a dive bar with grimy hard-wood and a stripper pole in the corner from some long-past incarnation. The clientele was all old men with large guts and 70s rock patches on leather jackets.

"I want you to show me the real deal here," Wade said, shaking with anger and too many cups of cheap gas station coffee, drank in an attempt to feel anything at all.

"Real deal?" Jim was smoking a cigarette and had a glass of whiskey nearby, not caring that the sun still shone.

"I know there's more to this then your links and articles, all that shit. I got into this to actually do stuff. I want to see it all, what you're doing to bring about this big change in the world order."

Jim was nodding again, grinning his jackal grin, face all lit up in spite of its sallow nature, its sliminess. "A man of action. I'll see what I can do."

Wade woke up to a pitch-black early morning with the buzzing of his cell phone. There was a message from a number he didn't know: Meet at the train station at 6 p.m. for transport.

Wade's brain, in a fog of sleep from dreams of disembowelings and skin-shedding beasts, began to register what he meant.

He told Roland Pettigrew in a brief email that he had it, that he would soon have results. Roland responded: OK, cool.

The train station was cast in the evening glow when he arrived, orange light on the brownish-red tiles, and Wade did not feel well-rested. People passed him, lost in their own business, and he twitched and startled at each of them. The slightest brush of air seemed to rattle him. His eyes felt tired again, buggy and dry.

The train was coming, the great roaring through the station. Looking around, Wade did not see who he was looking for. The train stopped, grinding on the rusted tracks, and people were lining up, bored, earphones in, books or phones at the ready.

Then the voice was at his ear. "Keep your head facing front," it said, a male voice, raspy but somewhat indistinct. "Don't look at me or make a scene right now."

And so he boarded the train with the shadow behind him.

The two of them, him and the man clad in black, wearing a face-mask, sat in the back of the train. The sun was a glaring orange ball against a dim sky now, and Wade could almost see the fire shooting off it in lazy, hazy waves.

"We're going to take this train out to Holland Station," the man said. Wade just nodded. He knew Holland Station was out in the rural area, the least-used station along the route, since most of the people moved out of the country decades ago. But occasionally you got a drifter or some unsavory types headed that way.

Wade felt a frog in his throat. They sat there like wax mannequins. Out the window, the evening faded to night, and the city sunk into the ground, leaving only rolling country plains and the occasional farm, fenced in and desolate in the darkness. Then even the farms were gone for a spell. The moon was out by now, and almost full. It looked like a glaring, bulbous white eyeball.

Finally, they got off and stood on the creaking wood of Holland Station, which county commissioners had lobbied to get declared a historic landmark, as it had been one of the first structures built in some godforsaken bygone age. Wade had been a patrolman then, in uniform and all, and he remembered having to attend the commemoration ceremony.

Now he stood on the platform facing out to miles of country.

"What now?" Wade finally asked.

"We wait," the man in the mask said. "There's a car coming."

"Okay, then," and they waited, listening to the cicadas and not much else. The air was crisp this time of year, just how Wade liked it. He thought of Lorelai. She had been into hiking, and this time of the year, when the winter had just faded, was the best time for that. They'd just been married when Wade had last stood here, at the commemoration ceremony. He remembered her telling him that morning that she was making beignets for dessert that night, and his stomach had been growling by then, 5 p.m. on a weekday listening to the hollow suits talking...

The car was coming up now, a black van. The sliding door was opening. The man in the mask put a bag over his head. "Got to be sure," he said.

The ride there was full of darkness and Wade lost track of time. He didn't know how much time passed, and, for a while, he thought this must be what purgatory felt like, timeless and neutral and cold.

Finally, they took the bag off his head. He blinked against the bright naked spotlights, erected on tall poles, which lined the road they went down. He craned his neck and could see a cave opening before them, a yawning dark maw.

Soon, they were down a slope and into the cavern, all the light, even from the moon, was now gone. It was a wide road, downward sloping in an easy manner, with rocky, jagged walls on both sides of them.

"Hell is this place?" Wade asked, his voice sounding weirdly small.

"Don't you worry yet," the man who'd met him initially said. "You're gonna see."

Then, after another indeterminate amount of time, they were into a wider part of the cave, the walls opening up to something that looked man-made. There were smoother roads and the walls were wider-spread-out.

Then another slope, and down deeper into the dark. The noise quality was odd. Even Wade's thoughts felt like they were echoing somehow.

Finally, all of the driving was done, and Wade could hear noise – human noise, like a kind of oasis in a desert feel, and they were coming to a man-made steel gateway, all shining black steel. There was a large congregation of people that Wade could see through the driver's window, many shirtless, many tattooed.

"Come on, then," the man in the mask said.

And they were at the gates and a man with heavy eyelids and a lip piercing was checking Wade's ID. He'd had it custom made and his cop ID, as well as anything else that could identify him as a cop, was gone, and the man with the lip piercing let him through.

Wade thought it odd to be judged by a man with a lip piercing, but then he reminded himself that this was a new world and the old norms were being thrown out, and it was probably a sign of his age that he was judging a man with a lip piercing, but then he remembered where he was and realized he was being silly.

The people were primarily centered around a large bare pit of rock. In the pit now, two men were walking up. One of them was heavy-set, but it was mostly muscle; the flabs not anything one would associate with sloth or over-eating, with long hair pulled into a bun. The other was lean and ripped, a spawn created of a gym somewhere. They met in the middle and shook hands. Then they began to go at one another. Punches flew with a speed Wade had only seen on MMA fights. Blood splashed to the ground and on each of the men. They grunted like primates, hitting bone and flesh and muscle. The crowd cheered as if it were the biggest sporting event of the year.

They separated, and the big man looked to be victorious, as he stood taller. But both were now bloodied, noses broken, cheeks and jaws swollen and disfigured, bodies hanging lower and bent like gravity was crushing them.

A single white tooth, reddened by violence, had come unhinged and now lay abandoned on the craggy rock.

Somewhere in the midst of the fighting, Jim showed up, arms crossed and a smug self-satisfied air about him.

"This is how we keep strong," Jim said. "We're breeding out the weakness in ourselves."

"Hell of a way to do it," Wade said.

"We don't half-ass anything, man," Jim said.

Wade nodded, feeling suddenly a bit nauseous. Another pair of men, this time both skinny like drug addicts, was readying. At the far side of the ring was a bespectacled, tubby man in a button-up shirt and khakis. He was sitting on an upturned bucket. He prepared a syringe, dripping with some viscous liquid. The two addict-looking men, the fighters, went to him wordlessly and stuck out their arms, and he injected them. Wade watched as they took steps back, closing their eyes as if reaching some kind of Nirvana. Wade thought it could've been his eyes playing tricks, but they had a kind of ethereal glow about them now, growing to cover all of them.

They stepped into the ring. The atmosphere shifted, as everyone was now looking upon them with a salacious interest. The two men stripped their shirts off and began to circle like hyenas. Others in the crowd were moving around, and then handing each of them small pocket-knives.

"Jesus," Wade said.

"Oh, this is the good part," Jim said, giddy, salivating.

The two men began dancing and weaving around one another. One of them, scrawnier, with more of a rat-like look in his eyes, thrust the knife. The other dodged, and then ducked low, thrusting his own knife, catching the rat-like man in the gut. Blood spurted out like a leaky faucet. The rat-like man let out a low guttural moan. The crowd was enraptured, the noise rising up from them was something euphoric and giddy.

More swiping of knives led to more flesh-tearing, more blood on the floor, little pools of red that shone under the bare lights that had been hung from the roof of the cave. There were cheers now, whooping and alien and cold, like they were watching a movie or some impersonal sporting event.

Finally it was over, as the rat-like man slumped over, blood and entrails leaking from him. A tall, broad-shouldered man in black entered the ring and dragged the body out and off to the opposite side of the cave, a trail of red blood now smeared upon the rocks.

"This is how we do it," said one man, better groomed than most in there, with a black jacket and slick hair like an 80s movie character. "This is how we take things back. How we fuckin' liberate ourselves."

Tremendous cheers, that rocked the cave, sounded. Wade felt caught up in something more than a sporting match now.

"They won't keep us down any longer," the man in the black jacket said, his voice big and booming like a broadcaster's, announcing this to everyone. "Our eyes are open. All of us together as one."

His voice was dwarfed, then, by the applause and cries.

"That's the guy," Jim said to Wade in the midst of it. "Our motherfuckin' leader, man."

Wade approached the man afterwards, offering a hand and introducing himself as his fake name, Hans. The man's name was Dyl

Radgewick, Wade learned, and he was the leader of the movement. He said he was a populist, that he didn't try to put any barriers between himself and the people. They were all moving towards the same goal after all, Dyl said.

"I like that," Wade said to him, sidling up like a fan of some rock star. "You've got a real thing about, like, unity going on here."

"That's what it is," Dyl said, grinning and showing off a set of pearly-white, perfectly-tailored teeth. "Everyone wants to divide us, to tell us what's what and get us on teams. I envision a world where that's no longer the case. I want a world where we are united by the truth and are strong enough to resist the corporate oppressors."

Wade nodded, unable to help the grin that was crossing his face. He hated to admit how good that sounded to him.

"Well, I'd say you're like a new Martin Luther King there, man," Wade said.

Dyl laughed – a booming, sonorous sound. "Well, I dunno if I'd go that far."

The hours seemed to bleed away from him, and then he was in a circle with Jim, Dyl, and two other guys, all of them drinking beer from cans. There were other conversations going on, but Wade was fixated on Dyl, who regaled them with a tale of how they had saved a convert recently, a woman who he called to join them. She was rail-thin, with hair the color of straw, but Wade thought she had a strong, defiant look that glowed through all her features.

"Suzy here, she was on the edge of losing it all," Dyl was saying. "Suicide. She was on the brink, lost her significant other, about to lose her job from cutbacks. But one of our friends, dear Aidan, was a neighbor of hers. And he saw her despair, and he persuaded her to come along to our meetings here."

"And it just... opened my eyes," the woman, Suzy, chimed in. "It showed me that there was something else."

"I took her under my wing," Dyl said. "And now she's a valued member of this resistance."

"And ready for what's coming," she said. In the dark her skin and eyes seemed to glower. She had a peculiar energy to her, Wade thought.

And Wade thought he might as well take the chance: "What is coming, anyway?"

"A revolution," Dyl said, smooth as butter, with the ease of suggesting they go to see a movie. "A total change of the order."

"Like, how, though?" Wade asked. He felt that he was on the edge of the truth here. But he needed more than vague declarations.

Dyl's face was neutral, but Jim was looking at him funny now.

"Maybe you ought to sit back a bit, man," Jim said, and it wasn't so much a request at all. "Maybe calm your pace there."

Jim caught up with him and put a hand on his shoulder as he was leaving the cave. Jim's face was no longer benevolent – or whatever had passed for it. Now he just looked cold, all hard features and skepticism.

"Man, you've been rubbin' me wrong tonight," he said.

Wade's smile was genuine then, although he had to hide the twinge of fear that came with it. "Hey, I got overeager. I'm sorry."

Jim nodded, but the coldness did not leave him. "We've had interlopers before. Instigators. We don't let 'em off easy."

"Look, I'm into what Dyl's saying," Wade said. "I like his vibe. I'm sorry for asking so many questions."

Jim nodded again. "Dyl's real suspicious of you. He ain't in the business of laying out his dirty laundry with new guys, but we let a lot of chuckleheads in here. Lost souls and such. Can't just turn 'em away. But you gave him some bad vibes."

"How can I fix it?" Wade was surprised to feel the desperation and smallness of one who had angered a lover or a parent – the eager tug in him to fix it now overcoming all else.

Jim smiled for the first time and it was the old snake-like quality in him, rising up again. "You gotta get in the ring, man."

Once in fourth grade Wade had gotten socked in the gut by a bully and had not managed the reserve to fight back. His father had said it was OK, that not everyone could fight, but the look in his eyes of vague and dismissive disappointment told him something else. That had been something of a spurious moment. He'd wanted to become a cop to harden himself after that, tired of his scrawny form, his weak attitude.

Now, in the office with Roland, relaying the tale, Roland said, "You don't have to do that. Come on, now. We've got our men, I told you."

"That's the only way to get anything on record," Wade said. "They let me into the cave for the fights, but anyone's allowed to see that. Far as I can see, they ain't doing anything illegal in the part I see. I know there's some other shit going on here."

Roland sighed and put his hands on his knees, looking down. When he looked up he had a somber look about him, eyes full of pity that Wade detested, that made him want to inflict terrible violence.

"You mentioned some kind of drug," Roland said. "A syringe?"

"Yeah, but we get 'em on that, and they skate by on everything else," Wade said. "We don't know what the fuck they've got in there yet."

"Hell, it isn't like we're asking you to kill yourself," Roland said. "You said you saw someone get stabbed in the gut?"

Wade felt his teeth grinding. "Yeah, well, what else do I have health insurance for anyway, right?"

There were two missed calls from Roland when he got on the train that night. And a text: I know what you're doing. Don't. Take as much time off as you want. But don't do this.

He ignored them all. The train went out to Holland Station again, only this time there was another passenger going there; a young guy in a baseball cap and a dirty gray hoodie and khaki shorts. He was totally nondescript otherwise, an average guy, zits on his face and all. He introduced himself as Martin.

"You're one of them too, huh?" he asked.

"One of who?"

"The seers," Martin said. "You know, the ones who see the conspiracy of it all. That we're being bamboozled."

Wade nodded. The guy was maybe college-aged, and he had a fervent look to him, cult-like. "Yeah, I'm headed out there. How'd you know?"

"I just got a sense," Martin said. "From the look of you."

They rode some more, and Martin talked about the only thing they had in common.

"It's so great to have found people who see through all the smoke and mirrors," Martin said. "Who see what's really going on. I'd hear the news talking about all this shit, and it's just like, oh, so I have to care about what you want me to care about now? I've got to just swallow your bullshit? And the politicians, man. Fucking leeches, them all. They act like it's a democracy but we know none of it matters. We know they rig everything."

Martin told Wade he was from a poor family and his mother was on medications, and said that tied into his reasons for joining the movement.

"All these leeches tryin' to make us pay out the ass for medicine to live," he said towards the end of the train ride. "Stamping on us with iron boots. Fuck 'em all, right? I want them to pay. I want to overthrow all of this."

"That's awful, about your mom," Wade said. He was thinking about a lot of things then. Threads in his mind were coming together.

Then they were at Holland Station and they waited amidst the cicadas.

The car was coming. And then the bags over heads. And soon the cave had embraced and swallowed them both once again.

He had stripped off his shirt and the cold cave air was on his chest and his arms, and he was painfully conscious now of how out of shape he was. In college, for a brief time, he'd had a six pack and had regularly

> **❝ Wade looked down at the black water, with the blood still there, and saw his reflection muddled and fractured as the ripples distorted it.**

worked out. That time was now long behind him. His opponent, it turned out, would be Martin, the young man from the train. The boy had a look of utter conviction about him, greater than anything Wade had ever known, a conviction that made him jealous, for Wade had never cared so damned much about anything.

"You sure you want to do this?" Wade asked. His mouth felt dry and his bones weak.

With no hesitation Martin nodded. "I'm up for it, man. Are you?"

Wade cast a glance in the crowd and caught Jim's eye. Jim with his skepticism back in full. Waiting for the shoe to drop, Wade thought, and so Wade said "I am."

They walked to the bespectacled man with the syringe, who told them to stick their arms out. Wade did so, and he watched the needle slide in, felt the sharp, acute pinch.

What happened after that was like nothing Wade had ever experienced. He felt a rush through him like whitewater rapids, and then there was an energy like he'd just chugged espresso, only more powerful. Everything looked clearer and sharper. He could see every detail in the stalactites of the cave, every curve and pore of the rocks, every bead of sweat on the people surrounding him with their hungry eyes, and all the sound was amplified, the chattering of spectators and the dripping water somewhere even deeper in the cave and the moonshine swishing in cups, all this symphony of activity, all frenetic and moving, and it made Wade's blood begin to pump. He was conscious now of his own heartbeat, as well. Ba-boom, ba-boom, it went; a flutter of growing intensity. He felt like he'd never have to sleep again.

Someone had handed him a knife. He was facing Martin on the other side of the circle and all of their cheers and jeers now surrounded them like smoke in a fire. Martin was dancing like an ape, his eyes black pits in the shadows. Wade began to move, too, and his movements came almost like he was being pulled by something, like a marionette.

Martin made the first thrust with his knife, and Wade dodged. Looking in Martin's face was like looking at a marble stone statue, no humanity at all. Wade shot his arm out lightning-quick, the knife extended. Martin moved just in time and Wade just made a scrape, blood now coating the blade, and Wade could smell it, entering his nostrils and further intoxicating him. The moonshine and the drugs and the blood, all in his veins now.

He stabbed again. This time he caught Martin in the thigh and Martin cried out, dropping his knife. The younger boy was clutching his leg and blood was spurting out. He was hobbling now, like a cripple. Wade watched this with the scientific precision of a man watching a bug under a microscope, and then he swept his own leg and cut Martin's good leg from under him, and then Martin was on his back and looking up at the cave ceiling, gasping for air, the blood flowing freely beneath him, pooling on the rocky cave floor.

Around them, everyone was whooping again like it was a big sports event, a game. Wade felt nausea floating into his conscience, a sort of tempering of the mania. God, he thought; there was so much blood.

But then Martin was getting up, trying to stand and reaching for his knife...

And the influence kicked back in like a second wave.

Wade knelt down over Martin and stuck him like a pig. Steel into flesh. Martin gasped and a blood-bubble formed at the corner of his mouth and his eyes were glazing over, as if he were seeing some other place, beyond this dank old cave. Wade pulled the knife from flesh with a sickly-wet thwack noise and there was blood and some guts coating it now, tarnishing the silver blade further. And the blood was on Wade now, too, and he felt that it was like some morbid sort of battle armor, or tribal tattoo.

Beneath him Martin gasped and the blood was running down his chin, and Wade looked at him and felt something like one of those cartoons on an island, because Martin looked so very delicious to him at that time...

And in one fell swoop Wade's body shot down and he bit off Martin's ear, flesh between teeth, the howls of the boy filling the cave and the blood on the ground fading into the background now.

He was nourished, spirit finally whole, and this feeling lasted only until the hand hit his shoulder and he was being led away from the ring.

Away from the crowd and the madness of it, there was a river and the man guiding him, who Wade began to realize was the man in the black mask from the first day, told him to wash off the blood.

His face, Wade finally saw, was as bland as they came; with rounded cheeks and a trim black goatee. He could've been anybody.

"Is the boy OK?" Wade asked.

"Just clean up," the man said. "You're filthy, now."

Wade disrobed, wading naked into the water. He let the blood wash off him and down into the darker recesses, to go unseen, the parts of the man fading away now, permanent and forever, and Wade pondered what he had done even though the full extent of it could not yet be seen.

Behind him, the sound of two hands clapping came, echoing through the silence of that part of the cave. Then there was Dyl's voice slithering through the dark toward him: "Congratulations, brother. You've been, transformed."

Wade turned to look at the other man, this enigma, and said, "Transformed into what?"

"You've lost all your inhibitions," Dyl said. "You've cast away the chains of this bullshit society around us, all the niceties and fake things they saddled you with, and become your true self."

Wade looked down at the black water, with the blood still there, and saw his reflection muddled and fractured as the ripples distorted it. "Well, shit," he said.

He dressed again in new clothes, a plain white shirt and khaki shorts and sandals, and then walked with Dyl around the perimeter of the crowd, where another fight was already starting, more whoops and demonic cheers as two more people got ready to destroy each other.

"Is the kid OK?" Wade asked.

"He'll be taken care of," was Dyl's only answer.

"So he's alive?" Wade asked.

Dyl didn't answer.

As Dyl turned away, and as the dark surrounded him, Wade sucked in his breath and took his chance. He ran into the darkness. He did not break into a full run, but a whispered half-jog, keeping close to the wall. He wished he'd had the foresight to do this before he'd been handed the white clothes, but such was life; it never went as planned.

Deeper into the cave he went. There was no one, amazingly, following him. Anyone could have, but no one was, and he was surrounded by the darkness. It was cold and the rocks were craggy. Without the bright lights of the arena, he was afraid he'd trip and fall, and if he did that then he would surely be found out, and he did not want to know what would happen then.

The cave began to narrow and the floor gradually became smoother. And then, up ahead, there were lights – dim orange torches, like something out of an Indiana Jones film, illuminating the dark walls and, further ahead, a large door. As Wade got closer he saw it was a smooth bronze door, and upon it lay a giant gold wolf's head knocker with eyes that seemed to menace him even though they were inanimate.

Wade's mistake was hesitation. He waited just a fraction of a moment and then there was a single set of footsteps running around the corner. Illuminated by the torches, Jim looked all business now, his serpentine grin gone.

"You fuck," he said. "What do you think you're doing, anyway?"

"It doesn't have to be a thing," Wade said. "Just turn around and go. You can still have your thing here."

"Fat chance," Jim said.

He was moving toward Wade like a panther, shoulders hunched, legs moving quick. Wade readied himself. When Jim was close, Wade threw a punch, catching Jim in the gut. Jim wheezed but didn't stop, coming at him with his longer arms, sweeping with his legs. They were caught in a flurry of fists and feet then. Jim, taller and lankier, was pummeling him with fists and kicking his knees and his shins and his gut.

Wade didn't even feel the blows. He knew he was bleeding and the kicks had knocked the air out of him, but it appeared the syringe drug was still in him at least a little. He felt no pain. He was on a high, pushing Jim back against the wall, driving his fist into the other man's head and neck. Jim coughed and sputtered but his eyes were still full of hate.

"You fucking interloper," Jim spat, blood dribbling down his chin. "Think you can come in here and just nose around?"

"Yes," Wade said, and with that he grasped the side of Jim's head and began to drive it into the wall. Like cracking an egg, he did this several times, and Jim emitted a series of pained shouts and grunts. Wade was afraid it would attract Dyl Radgewick, or the other goons. "Shut up," he hissed, though Jim was out of the realm of the conscious by then.

His body dropped to the floor, lifeless and twitching. Wade breathed heavy. What he'd done was right before him, but all he felt was a quiet, businesslike sense of accomplishment. Nobody else had come. Had Jim really just come alone, without alerting anyone?

He decided not to hesitate anymore. Stepping over Jim's lifeless, bloodied body, Wade approached the gold wolf's head knocker, and he pushed it and it came open.

He stepped into a room that looked much like the inside of a storage closet. The walls and floor were beige plaster and there were wood shelves protruding from the walls. A single bare lightbulb, shining a chipper yellow shade, hung by a string from the ceiling. Shelves were lined with plastic shipping containers. Inside those were rows of AR-15s and Berettas, shining black under the bare light.

Then, as Wade moved closer, he saw the last box, hidden beneath the shelf on the far wall. This one had several rows of yellow plastic C4 canisters, the cylindrical forms unassuming but, to Wade, deadly. He'd seen what they could do.

Jackpot, he thought. Hands shaking, mouth dry, Wade took out his phone and began snapping photos.

The fights were still going on when he returned to the entrance of the cave. The sounds of violence, the grunts, the slaps, and the gut-punches filled his ears and he felt a surprising jolt at his core. Flashes entered his mind of the knife entering the skin of the boy, Martin, and he saw it in slow-mo now, the steel piercing the flesh and the blood beginning its fountain-esque spurting. It gave him pause, slowed his gait. And as he slowed, he caught the eye of Dyl, who was circling the edge of the fight, and Dyl had suspicion in his eyes.

Wade sped up and was out of the cave. Above him the stars twinkled bright white and silver and the night sky was ribbons of indigo darkness, and there was no one else around.

Then the voice sounded from behind him: "You impressed me today."

It was Dyl. He had followed Wade outside, and at this, Wade felt a stab of the coldest and purest fear he'd ever known. But Dyl wore a benevolent smile on his face, and Wade wondered how good his poker face truly was, and if he was being bamboozled here.

"Thanks," Wade managed, the words coming out of him like molasses.

"You really want this, huh?" Dyl said. "To become one of us for real?"

"More than anything," Wade said, thinking of the pictures on his phone and the carnage the things in that room could cause.

Dyl nodded and a smile came over his face, charming and boyish, and Wade thought some people were just born for the role of a leader, and the kind of leader they were would be determined by their lives. And maybe Dyl had gone down some dark path unforeseen by his good looks.

"Well, keep coming around," Dyl said. "I think you're on a good path. I think you're the type of man we just might need."

Wade nodded. The van, to take passengers back to the train station, rolled up. Wade said, "I've got to head out. Work tomorrow, you know. The grind."

Dyl chuckled. "Indeed. Well, come back soon."

Wade boarded the van and the last thing he saw before the man inside put a hood over his head was a hurried foot soldier rushing up to Dyl, and Wade could not see them clearly, but it looked like Dyl's facial expression had changed to concern. Wade thought, had they found Jim's body?

But the hood was over his head. He knew better than to ask. The entire ride back, it seemed to Wade that time had slowed down. He felt like a bug in amber glass. He waited for the cold metal pressure of a gun to hit his temple. Every nerve was on fire.

But nothing happened, and he was deposited at the train station again, and he stood on the old wood under the bright crescent moon and listened to the cicadas. The train rolled and he boarded.

He drove home with wide, sleepless eyes, his joints stiff and veins on fire. A remnant of the drugs they'd fed him in the ring, he thought. Or maybe just plain exhaustion and terror, the reality of it settling in on him. And he craved nothing more than his own bed.

But when he pulled up to the stop light at his neighborhood he noticed the car behind him. Hadn't it been following him a little too long? He squinted at his rearview mirror, to try and see who was behind the wheel. It was futile, though; it was too dark and the car's windshield was smudged. The figure behind the wheel was an amorphous threatening blob.

Wade made a turn onto some unrelated street. The car followed, at a trudging pace.

He kept driving until he reached the Marriott Inn by the highway overpass. Its yellow lights were warm and he paid for the cheapest room available from the bored young man with the comb-over haircut who sat at the front desk.

Once in the hotel room he shut the blinds and moved the big chair in the corner of the room to block the door. He laid on top of the covers and slept a fitful, restless sleep. In the night, the patterns of that place, the cave, began to make more sense. He thought of everything in his life. A marriage that had faded until it was nothing anymore, a job that viewed him as expendable enough to send into the dregs. What, really, was he fighting for at all?

In the morning he got up and put on his shirt and pants and went to work, and there he told them all what he'd discovered, giving away the cave and everyone in it. They did not know the exact location of the cave, but based on what Wade told them, they had a pretty good idea of where it was, for really there were not too many options after all.

And then Wade would sit in the room and listen as the updates came in on the radio amidst the crackling static. An hour later, Dyl Radgewick, real name Dillon Johnson, was carted in, hands cuffed behind him, looking unspectacular in khaki pants and a baby-blue collared shirt, like he'd come from an office. Wade would soon learn that that was the case. They'd snatched him from his office down the road from at Aflac Insurance, where he worked as a pencil-pusher, invisible among the other drones.

In the interview room Dillon Johnson named three other co-

conspirators, who he said had been the real brains behind the whole thing. It didn't take much, at the end, for him to crack.

His co-workers would be on the news within a few hours of the arrest. Dillon had just been another guy they passed in the breakroom, sometimes told light jokes, they said. One woman said he had made a pass at her and she rejected him, and she had never quite liked the look of him after that. Some people swore up and down that they had always suspected something off about the man, and these would be the clips played over and over in the following days, painting the official Public Picture™ of the man behind the would-be orchestrated terrorism that the nation had averted.

Watching all of this made Wade feel a kind of emptiness, something foul flushed from his soul, and, as all this information flooded into, him he realized he barely knew who he was anymore. He walked outside in the sun and felt warmth on his face and could feel the cement beneath his feet and could hear the roar of traffic, all of these things suddenly immediate and close and loud.

Lorelai agreed to meet him at the Starbucks near her apartment, where they used to go after a round of sex or for a quick breakfast on weekends. He had memories of springtime mornings, dew on flowers, the smell of bold coffee in the sparkling weather, of her laughing at something that had happened at work, of her perfume, spicy and oceanic.

He was reminiscing on all of this when she arrived, hair in a bun, her face reserved. She sat with her legs crossed and her posture neutral. "So, what's up?" she asked.

"Well, I'd wanted to apologize," he said. "I feel it's my fault, what happened."

"Well, no kidding." She chuckled a little bit, unsure of his angle.

"Yeah, yeah. And it's just that I didn't see the forest for the trees, I guess. The job, it's a drain."

"Yeah, but that's not an excuse." She was looking at him as she often had at the end, stern and motherlike.

"I know. I ain't trying to win you back. I just thought I'd tell you that I get it. I understand I've destroyed us. And I was unfair in my anger toward you before, at the end of it all."

She nodded and they didn't speak for a moment, and suddenly she was averting her eyes and looked pensive, remorseful.

"What is it?" he asked.

"I'm seeing someone," she blurted out.

He felt as though he had been punched – the air in him seemed to contract until it was nothing at all really. "Oh."

"But hey," she said. "I'm happy you're doing better, realizing these things. You were unhealthy for a while."

"I know," he said.

She squinted at his face. "Okay, I have to ask... did you get beat up? You've got some cuts on your head."

He rubbed the side of his face, where there were some minor lacerations, relics from where Martin had caught him in their scuffle. "Yeah," he said. "Just a fight."

"A fight? Wow. So everything's OK, though?"

"Yeah. You know me. I've always been a badass."

"I've seen you avoid crushing a cockroach." She had a smirk again. Like the old days, even if just a ghost, a paltry remnant.

"Yeah, well..." But he could not think of the words to finish. He was reverting to older days, indeed, before he knew what it was like to stab a man in the gut, back to when he had known the meaning of hesitation and felt shame like an albatross.

There was something great and unsaid in his life now, an elephant in the room. At work he was hailed as a hero, but they also looked at him funny, like they were all wanting to ask the obvious thing: how'd you get as far as you did? Because there was no way a cop could've just walked in and gotten the information so easily. Not even the most skilled interrogator, wielding words like a weapon, could have done that, and so all of his colleagues looked at him funny. And he kept thinking they could see the ear he'd bitten off, or the stab-wounds he'd inflicted, and he ate lunch in the car a lot of days, staring at the passersby on the street, who did not have such inquisitive faces.

Online, he managed to track down Martin, whose full name was Martin David Puckett. His Facebook was a stew of links to blogs about werewolves and secret government laboratories. Halfway down the page he found another post: So fucking fed up with the world. Everyone's got their S.O. but I just get passed over and over again. Sorry I'm not jacked and can't play the guitar.

In Wade's inbox there were notifications from the obscure

messageboards he had been hounding in the early days of the investigation. They had not changed. More screamed obscenities against women and minorities and anyone else out of their peripheral. More theorizing that the feminist cabals were unifying in secret locations, pointing out men who threatened their world-view and plotting to have them secretly executed at a bunker way out in the middle of the Atlantic ocean. The Democratic senators were a part of this, they said. As were numerous Hollywood celebrities. It was the feminists who had to be stopped. It went on and on like this.

A buddy of his was able to track down Martin Puckett to a local hospital. He had been there a few days and no one had visited. Wade went to the store and picked up a tin of cookies and a case of beer, and as he was checking out, on the whim of the moment, told the cashier, "I'm visiting a friend, and figured this would all be good gifts."

The cashier looked bewildered and said, "Well, hope all of that goes well."

And he went to the hospital on shaky legs, like he was a nervous kid going to pick up his prom date. His prom date, incidentally, had been Lorelai. That was how long back their story spread, how sprawling their narrative.

He came to the room where Martin had been situated and suddenly he froze. The giddiness went out of him and was replaced with a kind of sickness that invaded every single pore of him, to the point where he felt like Medusa had given him a look, turning him into stone. He just stood there on the white tile as the mechanical voice came over the intercom, telling doctors where to go, announcing that visiting hours would be over in an hour.

A nurse with auburn hair tied back in a bun brushed past him and snapped him out of his trance. He'd had a habit of doing this; hesitating until the clock ran out, and then, whoops, guess he couldn't do the thing causing him so much anxiety after all, but this time he bit his lip and felt the pain. And it reminded him of the cave and of what he had done and why he was really here.

And he stepped into the room.

Martin Puckett looked smaller and more ordinary, somehow, here amidst the hospital machines and with the daylight coming in. He had a large bulging gauze-bandage where his right ear had once been, and it was a glaring thing, and he felt sorry that he had ruined this part of the boy's life. He'd never be able to go anywhere without people noticing that again.

The cave, Wade realized, had distorted everything. Everything in there had seemed so much more devilish, so much bigger and more dire, and Martin Puckett, this boy who he had mutilated, was just a 20-something outcast.

"So," Martin said, his face inscrutable. How was anyone supposed to handle a situation like this?

"I wanted to make amends," Wade said.

And he left the cookies and the beer on a chair near Martin's bed. Martin did not flinch away from him, but there was a sort of foul, standoffish look about him. Wade suspected it was his default look, the one he wore most days when he thought he had no expression at all. It was a curdled, mildly disappointed kind of glare; that of someone who had not had much in the world.

"I just wanted to say, if you need anything, you can call me," Wade said. "I work at the police station."

"A fucking cop, huh. A narc."

"Just making an offer, man."

Martin Puckett looked Wade in the eyes and it was like they had never left the ring. Like they still stood there with the jeering bloodthirsty hordes around them, and the absence of any law, and the lust the both of them had to commit murder during that bizarre and warped time...

"I bet I could take you this time," Martin said.

"I don't know if we should find out."

"You sure?"

And they were frozen there, inextricable from that moment that was now already in their past.

Snuff your truth to make room for my fire;
an infernal oasis for all thieves and liars and what they put me through.
A grieving pyre for all the shit I thought I had to do.
The flames lick my wounds inside this tomb, burning the nerves til it feels like a womb.
Born again.
Cremated in reverse, you made it so perverse by telling me things could be worse.
Like you've seen it all.
There will be no rise of a phoenix.
Hate to spoil the surprise, but I've seen this already—
I'm gonna fall
and stay down —hellbound and gagged to drown out the sound, lost,never found, and the cost of my honesty will astound.
I'm built from the ground down, growing closer to my demons.
The truth is under the dirt and ashes, it hurts and clashes with reason—
Never what I want to hear.
I see your logic and raise you my fear.
I see the killers, but I won't run. My rightful place is right here under the sun,
burning for you.
It's hunting season,
place your bets but don't waste your time.
I'm a shining beacon of a martyr in his prime, easy to find and out of my mind;
I'll sell my soul to the highest bidder, winner takes all; the whole bitter sinner nailed to the wall next to all the writing,
not fighting, not inciting the hate but inviting my fate,
undaunted.
It isn't love, but at least I'm most wanted,
and now this room feels less haunted—
I can see the eyes I was afraid of, they can see me and what I'm made of,
under all the shades of men I've been, and the one I'll pretend to be when I see you again;
good thing that good things must come to an end because
it means this is forever,
old friend.

#2

the reason I think
that I want to go to space
is to be in a place
that isn't a place—
nowhere
infinite enough
for me to stretch my arms
when you ask me
to demonstrate
how much I love you
and the lengths I'd go
to hold on
and hold in

i can only think of this
in terms of infinity
My affinity for you
limitless
ever expanding
from points in the past
to moving targets like
time—
endless and right
but fated by the finite

like me

But one day
in a billion years
when I am stardust
i will find my way to you
as I found you a billion years before
by the scent of your secret
and the glint of your divinity
beneath what was possible
love unrelenting
unbound and echoing
into eternity

#3

what if God already killed himself,
blew his brains out with a Big Bang
and all the celestial bodies
are bits of him
still spattering outward—
beautiful, wondrous things to be explored;

like comets

asteroids

planets

moons

and stars

but then there are black holes
invisible things;
the darkness God had inside him
that swallowed up the perfection—
spitting out twisted, frightful things to avoid;

like Earth

THE GIRL ON THE ROOF (PART 2)
BY DARRYL PICKETT

In the first installment, young teen Bud Manning met a girl at the Moon-lite Drive-In Theater. She seemed to know him, but he had no memory of who she was. Not knowing her name, he nonetheless enjoyed a romantic encounter with her on the roof of the snack bar, while his dad was unknowingly watching the night's horror double-feature. Curious and eager to return to the drive-in and get to know this mysterious girl, Bud has found himself in the middle of a dispute between his divorced parents. His dad will soon be moving out of state, and his mother's anger seems to have displaced her love for Bud. And now, the conclusion of the story.

Wednesday, November 12, 1958

Dad called on Wednesday night. He wanted to know if he could see me one more time before he left.

"He has school tomorrow, Everett." I heard Mom tell him. Even without hearing Dad's response, I knew what it must have been. "He has school every day. I only get to see him once."

She said no, but Dad showed up about an hour later. I heard the station wagon pull up outside. It was almost nine, and I was actually pretty sleepy.

"You want to go to the drive-in? Just once more. We won't get a chance for a long time."Mom stood in the entryway to the kitchen and stared at me, almost defying me to go.

"I can't, Dad. I have to go to school tomorrow. And it's late. Wouldn't be much to see."

Dad looked a little hurt by my answer. It wasn't the one I wanted to give. "Did your mother tell you that?"

"No, sir.

"I knew you would blame this on me." Mom stepped into the foyer.

"Jesus Christ, Lorna, it's the last time I'll get to see him for, hell, I don't even know how long it'll be." She looked away from him, biting back whatever hateful words she had formed in her mind. She tossed her hands in the air, walked past me and said, "Do whatever you want, Bud."

There was no right choice. Break my Dad's heart, or confirm my mom's worst suspicions about me. I knew that if I left the house, forgiveness would be a long time coming, and trust might never be returned to me. I followed Mom into the living room.

"Mom, I don't want to go out. I just wanna say goodbye. I don't want to make you mad."

She wouldn't look at me. She turned on the TV and stared at it, her mouth turned down in a grim, unreasoning scowl. Ridiculously cheerful melodies played from the television, a big band musical special.

"Mom?"

She had shut me out. I couldn't reason. I couldn't plead. All I could do was leave the room.

Dad had gone back out the door and was sitting on the front step.

"I'm sorry, Dad. I don't think I should go. Can we just talk here a while?

"Christ. I can't believe she's doing this."

"It's my choice, Dad. Don't blame Mom. Go to the back porch. I'll meet you there in a minute," I said.

I went into the kitchen and poured two iced teas, then took a sleeve of graham crackers out of the pantry and carried them out to the back porch.

I set the drinks and graham crackers on the small frosted glass table and pulled out the two woven plastic-back folding chairs.

"I really wanted to take you to the drive-in tonight," Dad said, breaking and biting into half of a cracker. He chased it down with a swig of Lipton and added, "I went there by myself, last Sunday. I wanted to actually watch the John Wayne movie."

"Yeah, we didn't exactly see it, did we."

"It pretty good. Anyway, I talked to your girlfriend." He smiled a little and then drained his glass of tea.

"What?"

"You heard me. She was working at the snack bar, just like you said. That's why I wanted to take you tonight. She was asking about you. She wanted to know why you never came to talk to her last Saturday."

"Are you serious?"

"I told her we were having a bad night. Told her I'd bring you by sometime soon."

"I still don't know her name. I don't suppose you found out."

"No. That's still up to you. She's a cutie. You should go talk to her. Get her number, call her up sometimes. Hey, the best romances are the long distance ones, right?"

He was smiling and laughing, and soon, so was I.

"So, can I change your mind about going tonight? We could get there for the last half of the second feature. Maybe get there in time to catch her."

I wanted to, God knows. I wanted to talk to her, learn her name. I wanted to kiss her again.

"I can't do it, Dad. Mom already thinks I hate her. She's got me all wrong, but if I go, I'm afraid I'll never get her back."

Dad stood, suddenly angry, ready to go inside and give Mom a piece of his mind.

"Don't, please! You'll just make it worse." He opened the door, and I said 'No!' loudly. It stopped him, and he backed away, then stepped out of the patio into the darkened back lawn.

"Then I better go before I get any madder. I'll write you as soon as I get to Kentucky."

He walked briskly around the house, back toward his car. I followed, almost running. I called out to him as he opened the door to the station wagon. He grabbed me in a tight embrace, and held me for half a minute, then sat down behind the wheel.

"Clarabel is over at Dee Backer's place. She says if you want you can come get her. Otherwise, she'll try to find a home for her."

"Dad..."

"I gotta go now. You'll hear from me soon." He started the engine and, in seconds, he was gone.

Thursday, November 19, 1958

I came downstairs the next morning and found Mom at the kitchen table, holding a cup of coffee. She hadn't prepared any breakfast for me, though

I saw that she had fixed two eggs and toast for herself. It was the first time that had ever happened. I didn't say anything. I got a bowl and a box of Wheaties and poured my own breakfast. I sat across from her, wondering if she would ever speak to me again.

"Why didn't you go with your father last night?"

"I told you why. I didn't want to make you mad. I just wanted to say goodbye."

"I wasn't mad at you. I was mad at him. I said you could do whatever you wanted."

But you didn't mean it, I thought. Anger was taking hold of me. I stood up. "I did the right thing!" I said.

"I knew you would hold this against me," She picked up a magazine and disappeared behind it.

INTERMISSION

July , 1961

This story needs to jump ahead a few years. After my dad moved away, I kept my head down, studied hard. I found my way onto the honor roll, and mostly stayed there. In my freshman year, I took up smoking, to counter the perception that I was a goody-two-shoes honor roll student. It made my mother furious, but she couldn't say much, because she smoked. I dated Jennie Caspars for a little while, but when you're fifteen without a car, you run the risk of losing your girlfriends to older boys with cars.

And boy, did I fall in love with cars, especially the following year, when I took an auto shop elective as a sophomore. The desire for a car of my own became an overwhelming imperative. I took a job at Winn Dixie and tried to save my money. When summer came, I helped out at Alvin's Garage for no pay. I took summer courses to stay ahead, and kept up my grades, though my school books were spotted with oil stains.

One Saturday afternoon, I came back from the garage to find a letter waiting for me on the kitchen counter. Mom had already opened the envelope herself, though it was addressed to me.

Bud,
I'd like it if you'd come up here to Kentucky. I have a good job now, and
I have been clean for over a year. Your momma told me about how great
you are doing in school and how much of a wiz you are with cars. I think
you could get a great job here and finish school too. It's something for you
to think about. I miss you every day.

Everett

It was a summons I knew I would get sooner or later. I was initially angry that it had been opened, but that faded with the revelation that they had spoken, and that she had said nice things about me. Our relationship had never really gotten any warmer.

When Mom got home from work that evening, she asked if I wanted to eat out at The Barbecue Pit, her treat. That had certainly never happened before.

We sat across from one another at one of the varnished wood tables on the patio at the restaurant "I got a raise at work," she told me. "Not that I can afford this extravagance very often, but I know you like barbecue."

I tried on a smile, and she smiled back. It felt strange, for both of us, I imagine.

"I don't know if you've made a decision or not," she said. "About that letter your father sent."

I had, but I didn't respond.

"I think it's the right thing. It would be good for you. And it would be good for Everett."

I was honestly shocked, not just because she approved, but because she said Dad's name without malice.

"I think so too," I said.

"I knew you would." She reached into her purse and took out an envelope.

"This hasn't been the best of times for us, Bud. I know that. But I'm proud of you." She pushed the envelope across the table. "It's a hundred dollars, Bud. If you're going to Kentucky, you're gonna need a car. So I hope this will help you get it."

I stood, moved to the other side of the table and hugged her.

"I'll come back for Christmas if you want."

"I'd like that,' she said, and kissed my cheek.

We spent the rest of the meal not saying much else, but it was a comfortable, peaceful quiet, nothing like the agonizing tension of the past few years.

That hundred dollars helped a lot. Before the month was out, I was able to buy a used Buick convertible that I had been fixing up at Alvin's Garage, with just that view in mind.

Two weeks into August, I had a license, a car, and a free night. I knew exactly where I wanted to go.

*****

Saturday, August 12 1961

Moon-Lite Drive-In Double Feature
The Pit and the Pendulum
The Creature From the Haunted Sea

The notion was a little crazy. I hadn't been to the Moon-Lite since that final miserable visit nearly three years ago. I had no real hope of seeing her there, but I knew I would regret not stopping by the Moonlite at least once before I left Florida. The drive along Highway 50 was a little nerve-wracking. I was a new driver, only halfway sure of where I was going. It had never been my job to navigate the route.

I still thought about her now and then, this stranger I had kissed but didn't know. From time to time, she showed up in my dreams, her face always shadowed, or lost in a glare. I set aside any notion that I might see her that night, and instead decided to remember how important the place had been for me, for my dad, even for Clarabel (still living with Dee Backer, older and slowing down, but happy, I was told by way of a phone call with Dad).

The Moon-Lite marquee appeared just ahead, flashing rapidly, two blocks away. There was a half hour of dusky light before showtime. I parked three rows back, then found my way to the Refreshment Center and bought a slice of pizza from the outdoor window. I glanced inside. There was nobody there that I recognized.

I sauntered around the building as I ate my pizza, folded in two atop a flimsy paper plate. I cast an idle glance or two up to the roof. I made my way back to the Buick in time for the first feature, and half-watched it, aware of how much less satisfying the experience was with only myself there to enjoy it.

I fell asleep before the movie ended, and woke up to a vision of cartoon sodas and candies dancing across the screen. I decided I'd buy myself a coffee and call it a night.

The menu board behind the counter had been replaced. It was now an aluminum framed display, lit from within by fluorescent tubes. Next to a Coca-Cola logo, it boasted in large red letters WORLD FAMOUS REFRESHMENTS. Quite a claim. Before I could join the line, someone approached me.

"Excuse me, is your name Bud?"

She looked about my age, blond, horn-rimmed glasses. Her sweater had the name Lyra helpfully stitched across it.

"Hi. Do I know you?"

"Nope. Somebody wants to talk to you. She saw you walk by a minute ago, and she asked me to chase you down since I was coming this way anyway."

The next moments were like a dream, as I followed Lyra down several rows as she led me to a red Lincoln. She opened the back door and hollered, "Okay, I found him for you."

There she was in the back seat, sitting next to an older boy.

"Bud? Is that you?" Her face was longer, less girlish. Her hair was styled up, much bigger and fuller than before, with a flip in the back. She smiled. "I couldn't believe it when I saw you go by."

"I haven't been here in a long time," I said. She opened the door and swung her legs around to get out of the car. The older boy shot a surly glance my way. "Where are *you* going now?" he said flatly.

"To get a soda. Do you all want anything?" No one answered, so she stood up, tugged at my arm and said, "Come walk with me."

She linked her elbow through mine and began walking, a lively vision in a flowered pink blouse and Capri pants.

"My, you've grown, Bud."

"Yeah, but you're still taller than me."

She stopped and glanced at the top of my head. "Sure enough. Don't take it hard. I'm taller than a lot of people."

In that moment, face to face, I had to check myself, try not to stare at her body, though for a moment or two, I clearly did. I brought my gaze back to her face, and was a little relieved to see she was decidedly checking me out as well.

"Well look at us," she said. "All grown up." We resumed walking. "How long ago did we have our little picnic on the roof?"

"When I was thirteen. I'm sixteen now."

"Three years? I can't believe it. And how can I be seventeen already?"

"Math."

She chuckled. "I always thought you were older than me, Bud. But math never was my subject. You here with your dad?"

"I drove here by myself. Dad lives in Kentucky. I'm moving there in a couple of weeks."

"Then thank goodness you came here tonight! I might never have seen you again!"

"Do you still work for your Uncle Vernon?"

"Nah. I got a job at Woolworths. My family only just moved back from Atlanta. I've been living there the last two years."

We stood in line at the counter, secretly glad that there was a little bit of a wait, because it gave us time to talk. I bragged a little about my car, and my grease monkey skills.

"That's good," she said. "There's always money in that."

"It keeps me out of trouble." I said.

"Now, there's something I'm no good at." She smiled shyly and her left hand traveled unconsciously down and touched the slight swell at her stomach. I didn't need to ask her what she meant.

A familiar sound rant out, a crackling electronic clucking noise. "Oh my God. The Lucky Cluck."

"You remember that, huh?"

"I fed a lot of money to that stupid plastic chicken. It never gave me the prize I wanted."

"You should have told me. I used to have the key to it. I even filled it up with those little plastic capsules sometimes."

"There used to be a spy camera," I said, and I launched into a monologue about my years of fruitless gambling, and my treasure box of useless knick-knacks.

She smiled and laughed. "You were doomed, Bud. I took that spy camera out of there myself as soon as it got here. You never had a chance."

"*YOU* had it?!"

"I still do. I even sent away for a tiny little roll of film. I think I took a couple of pictures with it. Never got them developed though."

"I don't believe it."

"Hey, you want it? I can bring it here some night and give it to you."

"I doubt I'll make it back." We were at the front of the line. It was my turn to order, but instead, I took her hand and began leading her out the door.

"Where are we going? Aren't you gonna get anything"

"Not yet." I said, and I continued to walk her around to the back of the building.

"Are you taking me where I think you're taking me," she said. I shot a smile at her, and she opened the back door, still warped and splintered. Soon, we were walking up the steps toward the booth. Vernon leaned out from his swivel chair perch.

"It's okay, Vernon. It's just me," she called out. He nodded and looked back to his projectors.

In another moment, we were on the roof again. She looked as if she was about to say something, but I placed my hand behind her head and drew her near. I kissed her, longingly and lovingly. It was probably as close to perfect as anything in life could ever be.

When it was over, there was a little silence. "I've been wanting to do that for a long time," I said to her.

"Thank you," she whispered and smiled, her eyes still closed and her face beaming in a way that I knew would haunt me forever. "That was the nicest thing I can remember in quite some time."

From the ground below, a girl's voice shouted. "What are you two doing up there?!" It was the girl with the name Lyra stitched on her sweater. "Campbell is startin' to get kinda ticked off. You better hope he doesn't see you up there!"

"I'll be down in a second, Lyra!"she yelled back. To me, she said, "I guess this is where I go back to my life. It's a little messed up right now." She held my hands in hers and smiled as she squeezed them gently. Then she let go, turned and disappeared through the door by the projection window. I followed, but she moved so swiftly down the steps, I never got another look at her face.

It went through my mind to shout out "Wait! Come with me!" But what was I going to do, take this stranger, worried and expecting, into my Buick

> **" She looked as if she was about to say something, but I placed my hand behind her head and drew her near.**

and drive her to Kentucky? I made my way down the sagging wooden stairs as quickly as I could. Once I stepped out the back door, I caught the blur of her shoulder disappearing around the corner. I hurried ahead to the main lot in time to see Lyra trotting along behind her, shouting that she never knew anyone so good at finding trouble.

I stayed put, watched their two shadows amble back to the car. From there, I could hear the sound of the Lincoln starting, intent on making an early exit, even as the laughably stupid monster in the second feature made an appearance onscreen. The car drove out of its lane and made a left turn to the path that went past the snack bar. I stepped out to watch it go by. I got a view of the driver's side, a skinny guy with glasses behind the wheel. From the back seat, I caught the glowering face of the boy who must have been Campbell, looking right at me. Once the car had passed, I stepped out to see the back of it, and there was her shadow, turned around in the back seat, one hand up and waving. The passing glare of snack bar lights on the rear window obscured her face. I raised my hand and waved at her vanishing shadow.

Five minutes later, I started up the Buick and left the Moon-Lite as well.

Lexington, Kentucky 1961

Kentucky was a big adjustment, for Dad and for me. I ended up taking two jobs in the first six months, and going to night school to get my GED. Dad fell off the wagon sometime after November, so I didn't get to go back to Greenlee Hills for Christmas. I wrote letters to Mom keeping her posted on everything that was happening. Once I had enough money to get Dad's phone hooked up, I even started calling her once a week.

Mom and I established a better rapport over long distance than we had ever shared under the same roof. We talked about my Dad, about better times long ago. I even told her about the drive-in, the elusive spy camera, and the mystery girl I had kissed. She was delighted to hear about all of it. She was the first to encourage me to start writing it all down.

Dad had pulled himself together again by the time I graduated, early and with honors. He was practically running the shop by himself, so I enrolled in engineering courses and worked my way to my first really well-paying jobs. Even after I could afford my own place, I stayed with him. He told me it was comforting to have me around. He reminded me every day how proud he was of me. His own health began a steady decline. In time, I quit the firm that had hired me and took over the shop myself.

Sometime late in 1963, I received a package from Mom. It had a familiar size and heft. My dad, by now spending more time in bed then out of it, was delighted to see that it contained my old Buster Brown shoebox, still holding all those dumb trinkets. Mom included a note.

I didn't really know what to do with this, but now it's yours to deal with. Can't wait to see you again soon. There is something else inside that I forgot about and should have sent you a long time ago. Love, Mom

Among the little toys was another box, very small, with my name and Mom's address. Inside, a small envelope, and within it, a note.

Bud,
I used the phonebook and looked up all the Mannings to find your address.

I even called your Mom and confirmed, and asked how you are. But I didn't tell her who it was. She says you might come back for Christmas next year. I'm having my baby in a month. I will go back to Atlanta and stay with my folks for that. I told you I would give you that camera. Here it is. Hope we can stay in touch.

She had drawn a heart. No name. But sure enough, there sat the camera, alongside its original egg capsule, and a tiny scroll of instructions. The lens was plastic, a little thicker than the body of the camera. A poorly applied decal on the front proclaimed WONDER SPY CAMERA Made In China. Six embossed stars surrounded the lens barrel. A small dial with an arrow showed where to advance the film. The shutter was on the side, a lever that did not click, but required the photographer to simply raise and lower it quickly. Per the instructions: *"shutter will staying open as long as is hold the lever. Many interest exposue effect made possible by there use."*

"Well, that's the damnedest thing yet," my dad said, and he laughed until coughing made him stop.

The camera and the box of treasures went into my closet, and I more or less forgot about them for ten years.

Lexington Kentucky, 1973

Emphysema took my Dad in December of '66. I went back to Florida for a while to stay with Mom. I enlisted in the Army Reserves, and I got sent to Vietnam in the Summer of '67. I served a six-month tour of duty. I was sent back after flying shrapnel tore my left shoulder. I have a medal and a lot of nightmares.

I live here in Lexington now with my wife Judith and my daughter Erin. I work at a small design and engineering firm just around the corner. I get to do some of my work at home, so I can spend time with Erin. She's almost four years old already.

Erin found the old shoebox last week and opened it up. She was delighted to find it full of toys. Judith asked me where on earth I had gotten such a variety of useless things. I've never mentioned them to her, or told her the story I've finally set down on these pages. Erin tried to eat one of the little dinosaurs. "These are too small for you to play with, honey," Judith told her as she sensibly took the box away.

A few nights ago, I pried open the back of the WONDER SPY CAMERA. I recalled a distant voice telling me, *"I even sent away for the tiny little roll of film. I think I took a couple of pictures."* The film was still in there, film that she had bought and used. I quickly shut the plastic door, hoping I hadn't overexposed it.

For the next few days, I couldn't stop thinking about it. Could those pictures be developed? Would she be in any of them? It didn't seem likely, but all the same, I took the camera over to Calvert Photo Shop. Mr. Calvert was kind of amused by the pitiful cheapness of the camera. "This is probably subminiature 16 mm black and white film. I'll do what I can with it, if you'll give me a couple of hours. I wouldn't expect much under the circumstances."

I met Judith for lunch. She wanted to know why I seemed so distracted. I told her I was nervous about an important contract with the city roads council, one of a thousand little white lies that make smooth the path of married life. I turned the subject to our daughter's upcoming birthday and our plans to visit Mom in St. Cloud over Christmas. Her face told me she had noticed the deflection, but she didn't press the matter. We left Stoller's Diner in opposite directions. I took a long walk and thought about events that hadn't occupied my mind for a very long time. How irrelevant it all looked from this distance. A few innocent kisses, a girl who was only mysterious because I had been afraid to ask her any questions. Still, what if her image showed up on that aged and mishandled film? The thought of it made me giddy, and that giddiness was a little troubling.

By the time I returned to pick up the photos, that feeling had me trembling a bit, like I was on my way to a rendezvous with an old lover, rather than just picking up photos that might not amount to anything.

"It's very hard to get good images from a toy camera like this," said Mr. Calvert."But I managed to print a couple of pictures. They're not very sharp, but you can tell what's in 'em."

In the first picture, a pickup truck rests next to a speaker stand, a shadowy figure seated behind the wheel, and a large, shaggy dog looking up from the flatbed. It looks ancient, an indistinct black and white mirage framed in a hazy black circle.

She is in the second photograph, her face and upper body in the frame. She's wearing a sweater, almost certainly the light blue sweater on which I once rested my head. Her hair is tied back with a dark ribbon. Her face is partially obscured by a flare of light, perhaps from the sun, and none of it is in sharp focus. The movie screen and the rows of speaker form a backdrop. It is clear she was standing on the roof of the snack bar when this picture was taken.

Every night since then, I've looked at her. The picture is faded and pale, lacking in detail, but how unlikely and how rare that it exists at all. This little window is the only glimpse I have. How I want to step through and talk to her again.

*****

Greenlee Hills, Florida, November 17, 1973

Moon-Lite Drive-In
Saturday Flea Market
5 am to 4 pm

I guess I've been writing these words to you all this time. I'm almost finished. This little notebook has been my secret. Once I get these last words down, I will put it aside. I'll try to stop thinking about you so much.

It's been a hard time. Judith and I struggle to keep things together for Erin. I hope we make it. I want us to work, as a couple, as a family. Judith knows I've gotten lost in my own past. All I know is my world changed too much, too quickly.

We are in Florida on our Christmas vacation. Judith, Erin, and Mom are visiting a theme park, and I have the day to myself. I knew I would come to the Moon-Lite, just to see it, even by day. Hooray for the Saturday Flea Market. In sunlight, it's drab, brown, and dusty. I guess drive-ins borrow most of their grandeur from the night sky. I'm still there now, sitting in my rental car as I jot down these final words. The building hasn't changed much at all. They're open right now, serving breakfast and lunch items to the flea-swappers.

I walked into the snack bar just a while ago. It was reassuringly familiar. I was greeted by a friendly, wiry little man with glasses and a nametag, JOHN. He's got a collection jar on the counter for a "Save the Drive-In" fund. He says the Moon-Lite will likely get bought out and turned into a shopping center unless the community saves it.

Your uncle Vernon is here too. He looks a little grayer, a little larger.

"I was just looking in," I told him. "I used to come out here all the time when I was a kid. With my Dad."

"Uh-huh." Vernon didn't look too impressed. "Anything I can do for you?"

"I knew your niece, I think she used to work here."

"Yeah. She sure did, back in, oh I suppose it had to be early sixties for a couple summers. You were a friend of hers, huh?"

"We used to watch movies from up on the roof here sometimes."

Vernon nodded. "I guess you heard what happened to her."

I had not. But instead of saying so, I just nodded and said, "Yeah." My instinct told me I would be sorry to know.

"It was a terrible thing to happen to someone so young." Vernon's face reflected his thoughts, and they were clearly painful.

"I'm so sorry," I said.

"Well, it was a long time ago." He smiled briefly at me, then he turned away, saying as he went, "John, give this guy anything he wants on the house." And Vernon was gone.

So this is it. I just ate the patty melt John was good enough to make for me. In just a minute, I'll head back in and put a twenty into the little jar on the counter.

I still don't know your name. I don't know what became of you. Did you live long enough to have your child? Did you secure a little happiness for yourself in whatever time you had? I hope so. Now and then, you still show up in my dreams, calling to me from someplace where I can't quite see you, from a hillside, a school stage, from the roof. I've studied your picture and tried to recreate you in my imagination. I remember your voice, and I remember how it felt to kiss you. I remember that more vividly than any other moment in my life. And these words are how I must bid goodbye to it.

Someone else may find this notebook and read it, and that's all right. I hope they enjoy it, but I wrote it to you. I'm leaving these pages, and the shoebox with its sorry treasures and the camera, and your pale haunted photograph. I'm leaving them on the floor just behind the Lucky Cluck.